Alex strolled into the room, dripping with confidence...

Ryder's heart shot up into his throat. She was wearing a sleeveless black dress that hugged every delicious curve of her body. She was as forbidden to him as any woman would ever be. The beloved sister of his best friend and business partner. There was no touching Alex.

And yet he had. Oh, hell yes, he had.

No one could *ever* know.

"Alex," he managed to say. "Hi."

She dropped down into one of the chairs opposite his desk and crossed her legs, sticking him with another tempting visual—her sun-kissed calves and lovely ankles. "Ryder." She forced a smile, which made her deep brown eyes light up, but there was something else there—fire. As in she would willingly set him ablaze if given the chance.

* * *

How to Fake a Wedding Date by Karen Booth is part of the Little Black Book of Secrets series.

Dear Reader,

It's hard to believe we've reached the conclusion of the Little Black Book of Secrets trilogy! This sexy series has centered on childhood best friends Chloe, Taylor and Alexandra, and an anonymous social media account that exposes the secrets of old money families like their own.

The heroine of this final book is Alexandra, and she needs a fake wedding date. Alex canceled her own million-dollar wedding a year ago, and the tabloids had a field day, which has made it impossible for her to start over—every guy in Manhattan is terrified they'll end up as the next headline. With Chloe getting hitched, Alex can't bear the thought of attending solo.

Cue Ryder, the best friend of Alex's brother. Ryder is the quintessential good guy, and he wants to help Alex, but he's worried about crossing the line with her. Spoiler alert: it's already happened once. These two will melt your heart! What about Little Black Book? We finally get some answers. No spoilers there...

I hope you've enjoyed this series! Drop me a line at karen@karenbooth.net and let me know what you think!

Karen

KAREN BOOTH

HOW TO FAKE A WEDDING DATE

HARLEQUIN®
DESIRE™

Recycling programs
for this product may
not exist in your area.

ISBN-13: 978-1-335-73575-1

How to Fake a Wedding Date

Copyright © 2022 by Karen Booth

For questions and comments about the quality of this book, please contact us at CustomerService@Harlequin.com.

Harlequin Enterprises ULC
22 Adelaide St. West, 41st Floor
Toronto, Ontario M5H 4E3, Canada
www.Harlequin.com

Printed in U.S.A.

Karen Booth is a Midwestern girl transplanted in the South, raised on '80s music and repeated readings of *Forever...* by Judy Blume. When she takes a break from the art of romance, she's listening to music with her college-age kids or sweet-talking her husband into making her a cocktail. Learn more about Karen at karenbooth.net.

Books by Karen Booth

Harlequin Desire

Blue Collar Billionaire

Little Black Book of Secrets

The Problem with Playboys
Black Tie Bachelor Bid
How to Fake a Wedding Date

The Sterling Wives

Once Forbidden, Twice Tempted
High Society Secrets
All He Wants for Christmas

Visit her Author Profile page at Harlequin.com, or karenbooth.net, for more titles.

You can also find Karen Booth on Facebook, along with other Harlequin Desire authors, at Facebook.com/harlequindesireauthors!

For Kim Matlock.
You've been supporting my books
from the early days, and I appreciate you
more than you know!

One

Alexandra Gold had a whole lot of reasons to need a break from weddings. After all, it had been only fourteen months since she'd called off her own. Logic said that she was still healing from the events of that day. Honestly, she still couldn't remember everything, but fragments played out like a bad movie in her head—the sobbing phone call to her mother, the long ride out to The Hamptons to return that ten-carat stunner of a ring to her fiancé, and of course, the tabloid nicknames she'd been given since then. *Ritzy Runaway Bride. Trust Fund Tornado.* And Alex's favorite, *Million-dollar Meltdown.*

She had every reason to despise weddings. But she didn't. They were a sign that hope and love were still thriving. Maybe not in Alex's life. But they were for others. Like her best friend Chloe Burnett.

"My mom suggested floating lanterns in the pool during the reception. What do you think?" Chloe, the bride-to-be, asked Alex over the phone.

Alex was sitting in the back of her black SUV on the way to lunch with her brother, Daniel. Outside the window, Manhattan went by in a hazy blur. August in the city could be insufferably hot, and they were in the midst of an epic heat wave. "I love that idea. They'll add so much ambiance. I don't know why I didn't think of that. I'll look into it." Alex put Chloe on speaker and typed herself a reminder in her phone.

"I don't know. I'm wondering if my mom is going too over-the-top."

"No. Moms are like that." Alex had firsthand experience with this. Her mother had gone overboard planning her wedding. And as Alex later found out, she'd been a little too involved in the proposal as well.

"Oh, God. I'm sorry," Chloe said. "I shouldn't have said that. I hope I didn't hurt your feelings."

Alex let out a heavy sigh. Yes, she had a difficult relationship with her mom, but that wasn't the reason Alex had called off the wedding. "Chloe, it's okay. I'm fine."

"But are you? Really? The last year has been hard for you. I'm sure it can't be easy helping me with my wedding."

"Don't worry about me. I love you and you're getting married. That's all that matters."

"I wouldn't ask if you weren't amazing at all of it."

"Aww. Thanks." Alex came by her talents for all of this honestly. Her mom spent the last thirty years as one of the most in-demand wedding planners in the northeast United States. Alex's exposure to countless matrimonial events led her to luxury floral design, and she'd built a big business creating extravagant arrangements for hotels, corporate events and yes, hundreds of walks down the aisle.

"Any luck finding a date for the wedding?" Chloe asked.

"No."

"I thought you met a guy last week?"

"And he figured out who I am, or I suppose more specifically *what* I am, which very quickly ended the conversation. As it does with all men these days. They won't even look at me. They just run in the other direction."

"That's so unfair. They don't know the real you. You aren't any of those things the tabloids said you are."

"You can't really blame these guys. None of them wants to end up in the papers, too. It can ruin people's lives."

"I'm amazed that you can even talk about it. You're so resilient."

Am I? Most of the time, Alex felt like she was putting on a show. "I'm trying."

"On the bright side, at least you canceled your wedding before Little Black Book appeared."

Little Black Book was an anonymous social media account that had cropped up a few months ago, peddling vicious gossip and family secrets of several people Alex knew, including Chloe and her mother. "I don't want to think about what they would dig up on me."

"Parker is really worried that whoever is behind it will sneak in to our wedding." Parker Sullivan was Chloe's fiancé, a sports agent whose star client had been the first target of Little Black Book. Chloe's crisis PR agency stepped in, Chloe and Parker fell in love, and all was eventually repaired, but Parker had been on a personal crusade to unmask Little Black Book ever since.

"I don't want you to worry about that. Taylor has all sorts of security installed at the house now." Taylor Klein was Chloe and Alex's other best friend. She was hosting the wedding at her family's summer estate in Connecticut. "Plus, you're keeping the guest list small, and you're inviting only very select press, right?"

"Yes. I couldn't keep the media away entirely. Otherwise, they'll have helicopters hovering above Taylor's backyard. But I invited a few publications. Ones I know I can trust."

Alex didn't want to say anything, but a few of Chloe's "trusted" members of the media had not been kind to Alex after the wedding debacle. They might not have called her the *Wicked Witch of Weddings*, but they had written about her, depicting her as the poor little rich girl. Alex didn't want to be pitied. She wanted to be left alone. Which was why she was so eager to find a date for Chloe's wedding—a gorgeous man she could dance with, so that the world, if they were paying attention, would think she'd quietly turned her life around.

The car pulled up outside the restaurant. "Hey, Chloe. I need to run. I'm meeting my brother for lunch."

"Do you want me to ask my mom to deal with the lanterns?"

"No. It's okay. I'll do it." Alex bid her goodbye to Chloe, hooked her handbag on her arm and hopped out of the car with a hand from her driver. Her brother was waiting just inside the restaurant's front door. "Hey, handsome," she said, standing on her tiptoes and pecking her brother on the cheek. His dark facial scruff scratched her chin.

"I see you're still wearing the sunglasses indoors." Daniel flagged down the hostess, then turned back to Alex.

"This is better. In case someone sees me. Everyone has a camera phone. This just cuts down on the odds that anyone will take a picture."

"Mr. Gold, we have your table ready," the hostess said to Daniel.

"Great." He stood to the side, waved his hand to

allow Alex to go first, then followed her into the dining room.

Alex looked straight ahead, ignoring the other diners. Luckily, it was pretty late for lunch and the restaurant wasn't overly packed. The hostess stopped at a corner booth, and Alex positioned herself so she could sit with her back to most of the restaurant, then removed her sunglasses.

"Can we bring you anything from the bar before your server arrives?" the hostess asked as she carefully set down two menus.

"Alex?" Daniel slid in across from her.

"Anything cold, preferably with a tiny kick," she answered.

"We have a lovely rosé by the glass," the hostess replied.

"Perfect."

"I'll have the same." Daniel folded his hands on the table, looking directly at her with his piercing blue eyes, highly focused. This had been his approach for the last year—take her out to lunch, probe for information about how she was doing, then report back to their parents. Dad was worried about Alex. Mom was disappointed. "So. Tell me the latest."

"Work is superbusy. I know it's a million degrees outside, but we're already staring down the holidays. I have a bunch of corporate events to do flowers for. And of course, weddings."

He reached for her hand and patted it softly.

"Good. Staying busy is good. I wish you had to do fewer weddings, though."

"Occupational hazard."

One of the waitstaff brought over their drink order. Alex took a long sip of the cool and crisp wine. It was exactly what she'd needed.

"How much are you helping Chloe?" he asked.

"A lot. I'm basically the de facto wedding planner."

"Who are you going with?"

Alex opened her menu and began perusing, although she already knew what she was going to get—Cobb salad, dressing on the side, no hardboiled eggs. "No one as of now. But I'm still looking."

"Looking how?"

"I have two options. Dating apps or getting a friend to set me up with someone."

"You aren't really doing online dating, are you? I hate the thought of that. What if you meet a guy who's a total creep? You can't get hurt again. I won't let that happen."

Daniel had always been protective of her, which was one of his more endearing qualities. He also felt some responsibility for what happened with her fiancé. He'd introduced Alex to him. "That's the modern dating landscape. If I don't do that, I have to wait for a friend to set me up and as of now, no one has found anyone who's willing to be seen with me."

"I'd offer to go with you, but I have a big meeting in London the week before and I'd planned to stay through the weekend. It would be murder to come all the way back early, but I'd do it for you."

Alex was about to blurt, "No way," but the waiter came by to take their lunch orders. So she sat on her words until he left. "I love you, but no. Taking my brother? I'd be better off going by myself. No offense."

He blew out a long breath and sat back in his seat. His lips were bunched up, his eyebrows drawn together like he was trying to sort out a complicated puzzle. She hated feeling like she was a predicament that needed to be fixed. "You need someone who already knows you. Someone who you can trust. Who I can trust." Just like that, his mouth fell open and his eyebrows returned to their original location. "Hold on. What about Ryder? He'd be perfect."

"What? No. Ryder? Really? No. He wouldn't want to go to a wedding with me." A pathetic, nervous titter leaked out of her. She downed the last of her wine. Was she sweating? Why was her heart beating so fast?

"Why not?"

Because Ryder Carson is my weakness. Because he's the guy I've wanted for more than a decade. Because he's your best friend and business partner. Because I secretly slept with him five months ago and I'm not sure my pride will ever recover. "I don't know. Just seems like he wouldn't want to."

"I don't think you should assume that. We should ask him." Her brother abruptly reached out and grabbed her forearm. "Oh, my God. I just thought of something. Ryder really is perfect."

"Perfect? No. I don't know what you're talking about, but you need to cut this out." Alex looped her finger in the air. "Whatever this is."

"Ryder and I have been trying to court Geoffrey Burnett. Chloe's uncle. I'm sure he'll be at the wedding. If Ryder is there and it's in a more relaxed setting, it could be the perfect opportunity for him to finally get him to come in and meet with us. So we can make our pitch and seal the deal."

Alex wanted to make a joke about how she wouldn't mind sealing the deal with Ryder one more time. But no. This whole thing was a very bad idea. She could only take so much humiliation in her life, secret or not. Ryder had really hurt her feelings when he'd sneaked off in the middle of the night without saying goodbye. Was there anything worse than having a door slammed in your face by the man you'd always wanted? "You want to use your own sister to cut a business deal?"

"If our architecture firm got Geoffrey Burnett's commercial development projects, we'd be set for years. We could buy a bigger office. Hire more people. And more important, we'd keep our competitors from getting that business." The look in his eyes softened. "But it's not just that. This is about protecting you and your heart. I can trust Ryder to not hurt you since he would never, ever try anything romantic. It's the best-case scenario for everyone."

Ummm... Alex cleared her throat. Her brother did *not* know Ryder as well as he thought he did.

"Did you say something?" he asked.

"Nothing. I think this is an absurd idea." *A painful idea. An absolutely ridiculous idea.*

"I thought you liked Ryder. You like him, don't you?"

Alex closed her eyes and hoped she wasn't going to go to hell for lying to her brother's face. "He's fine."

Ryder Carson was sitting at his desk in his office, trying to focus on the architectural plans that so greatly displeased him. They were for an office complex in Long Island, the sort of project Ryder typically conceived with ease, and always nailed on the first pass. But things hadn't gone his way this time. The client had a long list of wholesale changes they wanted, which could not be left to one of his staff architects. This was top-level problem-solving, and although Ryder loved the challenge, he wasn't happy about having fallen short. He did everything he could to do things perfectly the first time. Life was easier when there weren't messes to clean up.

Just as a headache was starting to brew, he heard a voice that made him look up from the plans. "Daniel, this is a goofy idea. Forget it. I need to get back to work."

Sheer panic struck him as he realized whose voice that was—Alex Gold, sister of Ryder's business partner, Daniel. His heart pounded fiercely. His palms began to feel clammy. He hadn't seen Alex since March, when they'd slept together. Nobody knew about it. *Nobody.* And with good reason. Alex's brother was more than Ryder's business partner. He was his best friend. And the success of Gold and Carson, the architecture firm they owned together, relied on the solid foundation between Daniel and him. Which brought him to the reason to be so damn nervous about seeing Alex. Because that night they slept together had ended when he sneaked out of her apartment while she slept.

"I promise it won't take long," Daniel said out in the hall. "Knock, knock." Daniel poked his head into Ryder's office. "Do you have a minute?"

Ryder's stomach sank to depths he didn't know were possible. "Is it just you?" He was fairly certain he knew the answer, but he wanted a second or two to prepare if he was about to face the woman who had every reason to be furious with him.

"No. Alex is with me." He waved her in.

Alex strolled into the room, chin held high, prompting Ryder's heart to shoot up into his throat. She was wearing a sleeveless black dress that hugged every delicious curve of her body. He could hardly believe he'd ever been able to touch her. She was as forbidden to him as any woman would ever be— the beloved sister of his best friend and business partner. The cherished daughter of the man who'd given Ryder and Daniel the money to start their architecture firm. There was no touching Alex. And he had. Oh, hell yes, he had. No one could *ever* know. "Alex," he managed as he stood. "Hi."

She dropped down into one of the chairs opposite his desk and crossed her legs, sticking him with another tempting visual—her sun-kissed calves and lovely ankles. "Ryder." She forced a smile and her deep brown eyes flickered with an intensity that was difficult to describe. The first word that came to mind was *fire*. As in she would willingly set him ablaze if given the chance. This wasn't the Alex he was accustomed to. She was a sweet and kind woman. Never before had she looked at him as if she wanted to shred him to pieces.

"It's good to see you, Alex. What brings you into the office?" Ryder asked, trying to get his bearings.

"I think I have a way to fix our Geoffrey Burnett problem and help Alex out of a predicament as well." Daniel walked up to Ryder's desk and stood next to it.

Alex shook her head in dismay. "It's a dumb idea. I'm sure you'll agree."

Ryder wasn't sure how he'd feel about whatever he was about to be pitched on, but he was still taken aback by her confrontational tone. It was clear to him that she was exactly as angry as he feared. Still, he wanted to know what they were going to suggest. "If it means we can fix our Geoffrey Burnett problem, I'm all ears."

"Here's the thing," Daniel said. "Alex is desperate for a date."

"Daniel," she snapped. "Do you have to put it that way?"

"Oh. Sorry. Alex *needs* a date. Really needs one."

"Hey. This idea of yours isn't just about me." She flipped her hand in her brother's direction. "You're the one who said you could use this opportunity for your big business deal. I'm sure you two care way more about that than anything else."

Ryder did care greatly about cutting a deal with Geoffrey Burnett, but he was confused how these two disparate ideas were connected. "A date?"

"Yes. To Chloe Burnett's wedding," Daniel said. "Alex is worried that if she doesn't have a date, the press will seize on that little fact and say cruel things about her in the papers again."

"You make it sound like I'm a fragile flower, Daniel, and I'm not. I just don't want to be stuck in their crosshairs anymore. My life would be much more pleasant if they moved on."

"And you thought of me for this assignment?" Ryder asked, incredulous.

"Yes. It's obvious, isn't it? I'm going to be in London the day before the wedding, so I can't go with her," Daniel said.

"He forgot to mention that I'm not going to take my brother," Alex interjected. "That will not have the desired effect."

"Right. I'm also lame. Have I mentioned that?"

Daniel's voice dripped with annoyance. "But I was thinking that we could have a real shot at Geoffrey's business if you can get some one-on-one time with him in a more relaxed setting. And I can trust you to take Alex to the wedding without anything happening."

"Right. Of course. Because it's Alex." *And you think I would never go there. Except that I already have.*

"Exactly. No romance," Daniel said as if that was a universal fact accepted by everyone. "Because you know that I would actually kill you. Our friendship would be over. And our business partnership ended."

"Mostly because you would be dead," Alex quipped.

"This is only because I love you both," Daniel countered with a noticeably heavy tone.

Ryder drew in a deep breath through his nose, looking at Alex, then at Daniel, and back again at Alex, which was a mistake because it was nearly impossible for him to tear his eyes off her. The thing was, he'd known Alex for a long time. And they got along great. For years and years, they had a comfortable friendship. In all honesty, he'd had very few romantic thoughts about her until the party at Daniel's last New Year's Eve when she kissed him as the ball dropped. Before that, he'd never allowed his brain to go there, precisely for the reasons Daniel had laid out. That kiss changed everything. It opened the floodgates. Which was why Ryder had broken away from it, grabbed his coat, and gotten out of Daniel's apartment as fast as he could. Before he could do something bad. Something that would ruin his life.

But then he and Alex ran into each other at a black-tie fundraiser in March. That night, Daniel was nowhere near them. In fact, he was out of town. More crucially, Alex looked like absolute heaven. She was being funny and charming and so sexy he could hardly see straight. That night, they gave in to temptation. It still haunted him. He had a verifiable weakness for her. He just hadn't known it until she'd forced the issue. Was he going to do nothing but make trouble for himself again if he agreed to this plan? "What exactly would this entail?"

"Well, you'd just do your best to get as much time with Geoffrey Burnett as you can." Daniel turned to Alex. "Alex will need to be there for the rehearsal dinner, the ceremony and reception, so you'll have plenty of opportunity to talk to him."

That wasn't what Ryder meant when he'd asked the question, but perhaps two separate conversations needed to take place—the business one with Daniel and the personal one with Alex. "I can do that." Ryder was terrible with small talk, but in his experience, real estate developers loved discussing their projects and the architecture involved. He could go on about that for hours. "And I think you're probably right. This could give us an edge over the other firms who are vying for this business."

"It will give us a huge advantage," Daniel said.

That much was sewn up. Now to the other issue at hand. "I think we need to find out what Alex wants from this scenario. That's more important than the business aspect of it." Ryder looked at Alex and there was a moment when their gazes connected and he saw a glimmer of the woman who tempted him with her softness and vulnerability. The woman who wasn't angry with him. This glimpse scared him, but it also pulled on his heartstrings like nothing else. He felt so bad about everything she'd been through in the last year. If being her date would help her at all, he was willing to do that.

"Thank you for acknowledging me in all of this," Alex said, casting an annoyed glance at her brother, then returning her attention to Ryder. "You need to pretend to like me for three days. Act like you're my boyfriend."

"Nothing too over-the-top," Daniel added.

"Will you let me finish?" Alex pleaded. "I just need you to be a solid but unobtrusive presence. The handsome guy who holds my hand and brings me a drink. But who doesn't draw a lot of attention."

Ryder had to hide his smile. It was nice to hear her say that she thought he was handsome. "I can do that."

"See? This is perfect." Daniel's phone buzzed, and he pulled it out of his pants pocket. "I need to go. But you two can work out the specifics, right?"

"Yes. We're capable of that much." Alex got up

from her chair and hugged her brother goodbye. "Thanks for lunch. And thanks for having my back."

"Of course. Always."

Ryder had witnessed the affection between these two many times. It was a big part of the reason why he'd never seen Alex as more than a friend. Ryder was an only child. He didn't have that kind of relationship in his life. And from the looks of it, he'd missed out. Big-time.

Daniel excused himself, leaving Alex and Ryder alone. Granted, the door to his office was wide-open, but it still put him on edge. "I didn't see this coming."

"Me neither." She sighed and scanned his face, seeming doubtful. "You can say no if you want. It's not too late to back out."

Ryder felt as though he was being dragged in opposing directions. He and Daniel had a whole pile of reasons they needed Geoffrey Burnett's business. And he couldn't *not* help Alex if she needed it. But did he trust himself to not touch her? To not kiss her? Not really. "I'm not going to back out."

"Let me remind you that we have some history that could make this difficult. Although I suppose one could argue that the note you left me in the middle of the night shut the door on that."

Ryder stepped out from behind his desk and shoved his hands into his pockets. "I'm sorry about leaving. Really. I am. I just thought it was best for all involved. You, me and your brother. It's too complicated. And considering everything you've been through, the last thing you need is complicated."

She hesitated for a moment, then eventually nodded. "You're right."

"So? What now?"

"I thought about it in the car over here from the restaurant. I don't think we can just show up at the wedding together and act like we're a couple. The press has a nose for fake relationships, and if they suspect that, they'll skewer me again."

"How do we get around that?"

"Two things. First, a date. In the city. I'll get Chloe to tip off the press. They can see us together and think it's the start of something."

"What's the second thing?"

"Right now, you walk me downstairs and kiss me goodbye out on the street. Just to get the ball rolling."

He swallowed hard. "Okay…"

"Come on. I'm sure you remember how to do it." She hooked her handbag on her arm and started for the door.

Ryder dutifully followed her out into the hall, down to Reception and to the elevator. All along, he had to wonder how Alex knew that these were the right things to do. Had she been planning this? That seemed improbable. It certainly wouldn't account for her brother's role in all of this. The elevator dinged and they climbed on board to take it to the ground floor.

"We can take care of this, then the date, and it'll seem like no big deal when we get to the wedding."

"And that's your hope? That it seems like no big deal?" he asked.

"Exactly."

Could it possibly be that easy? "Okay, then. When and where for our date?" The elevator door slid open and they started through the lobby.

"Next Thursday. The day before the wedding weekend," Alex said. "I'll call you with the time and place."

"You have my number, right?" He followed her through the revolving doors of his office building. The heavy August air was insufferable from the word go, doing nothing to alleviate his nervousness about this kiss. The heat had been turned up, for real.

Alex came to a stop on the sidewalk. "Yes, I still have your number. Even after you left me that horrid note."

He reached for her arm, and the connection between them hit him square in the center of his chest. He couldn't see the force, but he could feel it, and it shook him to his core. He regretted hurting her by leaving, but sometimes life gave you difficult choices and he was certain that in that instance, he'd made the right one. "I'm sorry, Alex. I really am."

"I'm sure. Let's just get this over with." Without wasting so much as a second, she gripped his biceps, leaned into him and planted her lips on his. It was as if the world tilted off its axis and hurtled

Ryder through space. Just as he started to kiss her back, she pulled away, leaving his mouth buzzing, his body even hotter than the air around him. "I'll text you, Ryder."

"Alex, that note was for your own good. I believe that."

She pulled her sunglasses out of her bag and slid them onto her beautiful face. "Well then that's perfect. Because that's the only thing I'm worrying about anymore."

Two

Thursdays at Alex's floral studio, Flora, were for designing. The entire place buzzed with frenetic energy, her staff preparing for the Friday push and eventually the crush of their biggest moneymaker—weddings. Today was a special Thursday, though. She'd personally done all of the arrangements and bouquets for Chloe's wedding a day early since she'd be traveling to Connecticut with Ryder tomorrow. She spent the entire day in the back surrounded by large wooden benches where her battalion of designers worked. That morning, the floor had been packed with buckets of blooms, but now that it was late afternoon, their stock had been fully depleted. Even so, the heavenly scent of fresh-cut freesia, roses and magnolias hung in the air.

Alex was spent, but satisfied with everything for the wedding. It was all to be kept in the coolers overnight, then one of her delivery drivers would bring it all up to Taylor's family's estate in Connecticut tomorrow. Now her biggest thing to prepare for was her date with Ryder tonight. The kiss she'd given him the other day was still in her head *and* on her lips. She kept seeing flashes of that moment out on the sidewalk, and it didn't take much to push her from that vision to memories of their one smoking-hot night together. Why did he have to be so steadfast in his devotion to her brother? She admired him for it, but it was the number one thing standing in her way.

Alex's most prized employee, Jade, walked into the studio from the retail side of their space, on 28th Street. "Alex, we're completely sold out, so I'm about to close up and go for the day, unless you need anything."

"What time is it?" Alex looked up at the clock on the wall. It was four thirty. She'd thought it was closer to four. Ryder was set to meet her here any minute now and she was a wreck. "Actually, can you hang out in the front while I change and fix my makeup? Someone is meeting me here. It shouldn't be long before he gets here."

"Ooh. Hot date?"

The guy is hot. The date will be decidedly chaste,

except for the part where we purposely get busted by the tabloids, kissing. "Not exactly."

The recognizable chime on the shop door sounded. Jade grinned and glanced back through the entrance from where she'd come, then turned back to Alex. "Very nice. And tall. I love a tall guy," she muttered with a bounce of her eyebrows.

"Oh, God. He's here?"

"I can only assume. Most people don't arrive with flowers. They usually walk out with them."

Flowers? As panicked as Alex was about the way she looked right now, her heart still flipped at the thought of seeing Ryder, especially since he'd thought to bring a gift. And a romantic one at that. Maybe this wouldn't be as painful as she'd feared. "I'll go talk to him and you can head home. I'll lock up."

"You sure?"

"Yep."

"Okay. You can tell me about the date later."

"Believe me, there won't be much to tell." Alex rushed past Jade and into the shop. Sure enough, there stood Ryder in the center of the room.

He was dressed in an impeccable gray suit that accentuated the strong lines of his towering frame. He was a vision plucked straight out of her fantasies, clutching a simple but elegant bouquet of white tulips. "Won't be much to tell about what?" The tone of his chocolate-brown eyes was especially warm right now, brought out by the dark scruff along his jawline. As she stepped closer to him, his shoulders nearly blocked out the late-day sun.

"Oh, nothing."

"Hmm." Seeming unconvinced, he frowned, which somehow made him even more handsome. "I brought flowers. Which I realize was probably a poor choice given your occupation, but I didn't want to come empty-handed. Also, I felt like a real apology was in order." He handed her the bundle of blooms, which was wrapped in brown craft paper, tied with a wide white-satin bow.

"Where did you get these?"

"From the florist near our office."

"They're very nice. Thank you." Funny, but even with her immense love for flowers and her rich fantasy life when it came to Ryder, she'd never imagined this particular scene. Knowing how little chance she had at a romantic future with him, it was probably a good thing. "White was a good choice. It sends the right message."

"I chose them because they looked the best out of what they had."

"Well, the color of flowers is significant. White can mean purity and innocence."

He cocked an eyebrow at her. "That doesn't seem quite right given our history."

Her cheeks plumed with heat. "But it can also mean reverence and humility."

"Okay, good. Because I'm serious about that apology." He glanced at the doorway leading to the back room. "Are we alone?"

She had to smile at the question. Was he nervous? If so, she liked it. So often she felt like she was off her game when she was around him. "We are."

He cleared his throat and folded his hands in front of him, as if he was about to plead his case. "The way I left in the middle of the night was wrong. But I also knew that what happened between us wasn't right, either."

What little bit of optimism the flowers had given her was now gone. She hated hearing him cast their night together in that way, as a mistake. "Because of my brother."

"Yes, but it's more than that. You've been through a lot. I should never have let that happen."

"The last year has been hard, but I'm not broken, Ryder." Yes, he'd hurt her feelings when he'd left, but she'd lived with plenty of disappointment, especially over the last twelve months. It was just one more thing to add to the pile. And she still wanted to think of their one night together as a false start, rather than Ryder successfully closing the door on the idea of them. Despite her brother putting up roadblocks, she still wanted to believe that she and Ryder could find a way. How that might happen, she didn't know, but she wasn't ready to put it in the category of impossible.

"That may be true, but I also don't want to be the reason you break."

Alex nodded, fighting back the frustration that was already building in her body. She knew she shouldn't be angry with him when he was being a good guy, but being a "good guy" meant that she couldn't have what she really wanted—him. "I should probably change so we can get out of here." She stepped to the long counter where the register sat and put down the flowers he'd brought, then reached back to untie the apron she'd worn all day.

"For what it's worth, I think you look great."

She glanced down at herself. She was wearing slim black pants and a matching tank top, her usual workroom attire in the middle of the summer. "Not exactly the height of fashion."

He cleared his throat again, but this time stuffed his hands into his pockets. "I wasn't talking about what you're wearing."

She froze as a wave of indescribable heat climbed from her feet straight up to her face. Good Lord, tonight was going to be especially difficult if he was going to say things like that. She needed to prepare herself for an evening of choking back the real words she wanted to say. Things like, *Stop being a good guy and take me on the counter next to the register, already.* "It'll just take me a minute to change."

"Okay. I'll wait."

She rushed upstairs to her office, grabbed her makeup bag from her purse and ducked into her bathroom. It was too hot out to do much more than swipe on an extra coat of mascara and a light coat of lipstick. Blush certainly wasn't needed. A few minutes with Ryder and her cheeks were already ripe with color. She kicked off the sneakers she'd worn all day, ditched her work clothes for a black sleeveless wrap dress that she worried Ryder wouldn't notice. It wasn't so much that she was trying to entice him, so much as she wanted to remind him of what he could have, if only he was willing to bend a few rules with her brother.

After working her feet into a pair of strappy sandals, she met Ryder back downstairs. The instant when he saw her and his eyes flashed with approval was enough to tell her that she'd done the right thing with her wardrobe choice. At least she could feel good about herself while Ryder was only pretending to like her in a romantic way.

"Where are we off to?" he asked.

"I asked you to come on the early side so we can see some art at the Whitney before they close. Then I was thinking we'd grab a cocktail and a bite to eat at the rooftop steak place up the street from there. After that, a walk on the High Line. That's where Chloe has the photographer staked out. He'll be there around eight thirty."

"Sounds to me like you have it all figured out."

If only he knew how little work it had taken her to come up with a plan. This was the sort of night she'd dreamed of many times, doing all of her favorite things with the guy she wanted so badly. It was a sad state of affairs that it had to happen under these fake circumstances, but there was no point in lamenting the fact. She needed to be happy with what she had ahead of her—a few hours with Ryder Carson. And after that, a whole weekend, when her brother would be an ocean away.

Ryder and Alex made it to the Whitney about an hour before closing. She took his hand the instant they were inside, and neither let go as they strolled through the galleries, admiring the vast array of modern art.

"Thoughts on this one?" Alex asked as she stopped in front of a painting by Charles Demuth. The work had a remarkably contemporary feel for something created in the 1920s—angular rays of sunlight shining down on a steely gray building, with a color-blocked blue sky above and the same geometric treatment for the rusty earth below.

"I love it. Is it one of your favorites?"

She considered it again, with her head tilted to one side. It was impossible to keep from admiring her beauty, the way her tumbling hair contrasted with her lightly sun-kissed complexion. "I love it, too. I thought you would appreciate the light and dark. You seem like a very black-and-white thinker to me. One thing is good. Another thing is bad."

Ryder wasn't sure whether he should be offended. People with that take on the world weren't always the most open-minded and he considered himself to be a nonjudgmental person. "I don't think that's true. At all."

"Well, maybe it's that you like absolutes. Guarantees."

What exactly was wrong with that? In Ryder's mind, certainty was too rare a commodity. "If you mean that I like being able to count on things, then sure. It's part of why I went into architecture. It's a marriage of precision and artistry, but you end up with something solid and concrete. I can look at one of my designs when construction is complete and say that I pulled the idea out of thin air, but it's built to last. There's a lot of nuance to that process."

Alex slid him a questioning look. "Are you saying that I'm not giving you enough credit?"

He tugged on her hand so they could keep looking. "No. I don't care about credit. I'm only saying that I don't want you going around thinking you have me completely figured out."

"I've got you at least a little bit figured out."

He couldn't help but smile. The night they'd slept together, she'd certainly figured out what could make him happy on a physical level. "Remind me to surprise you at some point."

They left the Whitney at six when they closed, then walked over to the restaurant, which was only a block or so away. A thunderstorm had come through while they were in the museum, and the sidewalks were dark with moisture while wisps of steam from rain hitting hot asphalt curled into the air. The temperature had dropped nearly ten degrees, a welcome reprieve from the August heat, but the air held on to that sweet summer stickiness. They held hands for the entire walk. Ryder could admit to himself that he did like the excuse of having Alex as a fake girlfriend. No, this wasn't real. But it felt good. It also felt comfortable, which he realized wasn't a particularly sexy descriptor for a boyfriend-girlfriend arrangement. But when he didn't have to wrestle with his desire for her too much, and he could let down his guard, he loved that he didn't have to put on a show with her, even when that was exactly what they were doing for the rest of the world.

At the restaurant, they headed up to the rooftop patio, which had an amazing open-air bar with string lights zigzagging overhead and the buzz of a big crowd. Ryder would have preferred a quieter setting, but he understood what tonight was about—being seen together. They did manage to get a corner table with near-panoramic views of the neighborhood, so that was a good thing. After ordering drinks—a margarita for Alex and a beer for Ryder, as well as a few appetizers, Ryder felt that it was time for him to once again bring up the subject he didn't want to discuss, but which he knew must be addressed before they went away for the weekend. They needed a solid foundation between them, with clear boundaries and zero gray area.

"Alex. I feel like we need to talk about the note.

And our night. Or at least I feel like I need to explain myself fully."

She arched both eyebrows at him and sat back in her seat, crossing her arms over her chest. The night air blew a lock of hair across her cheek, which she brushed away. "Go ahead. Explain away."

He cleared his throat, preparing to run through the points he'd mulled over in his mind many times. "I don't take my friendship and my partnership with your brother lightly. And it's not that I regret what happened between us, but I do regret the weakness I showed when I gave in to temptation."

"So you're saying I'm tempting?" she interrupted.

"No." He shook his head. "I mean, yes. Of course you are. But that's not my point. My point is that the moment of weakness is the reason I left without saying goodbye. In my mind, there was nothing to discuss. I'd crossed a line I should never have considered crossing. And the sooner I could start rectifying the situation, the better, which was why I didn't wait until morning."

She nodded, seeming extremely skeptical of his explanation. "Right. Because if we'd had a conversation, I might have been able to convince you that you were wrong. And then where would you have been? In trouble with Daniel."

"It's not about being in trouble, Alex. I don't want you to think I'm not my own person." He leaned closer so he could speak in a softer tone. "But you're going through the aftermath of a very traumatic event. And I don't really do serious. So it was never going to end well. I'm supposed to sacrifice my relationship with your brother for something that would likely end badly?"

She scrunched up her lips. "Sounds like some very black-and-white thinking."

He took a long swig of his beer and flagged down the waiter. "Another round, please." He looked at Alex. "Unless you don't want another."

"Oh, I'm having *so* much fun, Ryder. I can't wait to have another drink." Her voice dripped with sarcasm. This was officially going as badly as it possibly could.

"Look," Ryder said when the waiter left. "This is the reality of our situation. There's nothing wrong with accepting things as they are. If you think about it, it's really the smartest thing to do."

"Okay, then. Why don't you tell me the reality of why you don't do serious? Because it doesn't jive with your personality at all. You're a good friend. You're very loyal. And you're also known for being dependable. I know you care about your family a great deal. Don't you basically support your dad?"

That stopped Ryder dead in his tracks. He rarely discussed his family, mostly because there was never anything good to say. He loved his father, but the man was incredibly difficult. When Ryder was growing up in Boston, his family unit consisted of only his grandmother and dad. Ryder's mom had passed away right after he was born. Dad worked construction while Grandma had played the role of mom. The three of them got by, but things were always tight. There were times when the electricity was shut off or there wasn't money for groceries. That's why it had been so important for Ryder to succeed, do it quickly and to do it on a large scale. It had always been his ultimate goal to help his family have stability. Ultimately, he was too late with his grandmother. She died before he could do anything more than pay her medical bills. His dad was another story.

"I try to help my dad. He doesn't always accept the money. He's very proud. It took me a good five years of pleading with him before he let me fix up his house and pay off his mortgage."

"Like I said, you're a good person. So why don't you do serious when it comes to relationships?"

"I don't really have time. Work comes first now. And before that, it was school." Daniel joked about Ryder being a love 'em and leave 'em sort of guy, but that wasn't the truth. Ryder simply hadn't met a woman that meant more to him than achieving his professional goals. The one exception could've been Alex, but he'd told himself from the beginning that he wouldn't go there. Ryder always kept promises to himself. He knew he was the one person he could count on.

The waiter delivered their second round, giving Ryder a short respite from the conversation, where he felt as though he'd managed to put himself on the spot. He should have stuck to lighter topics like the weather or what the color of various flowers meant. For now, since things were already uncomfortable between Alex and him, he decided he'd better bring up the other topic he'd been avoiding. "Can I ask what the sleeping arrangements will be during the wedding?" He didn't want to be caught off guard when they got to Connecticut. Unfortunately, the delay in a response from Alex told him exactly how she felt about his inquiry—she disliked it, greatly.

"I figured you were going to ask me about that."

"It's a legitimate question. Your brother's presence is looming over all of this, Alex."

"As if I don't already know that." She licked salt from the rim of her glass, momentarily making him wish he could be a grain of salt. "I spoke to Taylor and one of the guest rooms has two beds. So we'll be sharing a room, but there will be separate beds."

Ryder exhaled. That wasn't ideal, but he could live with that. He and Alex would still be spending copious amounts of time together, which wouldn't be easy to endure, but at least they wouldn't have to sleep next to each other. "Okay. Great."

"Do you need to report that to Daniel? Or should I?"

Ryder shook his head. "Alex, come on. Surely you care just as much about your brother as I do. And probably more."

She rattled the ice in her glass then took a final sip of her drink. "I love him to death, even though his stubborn ideas about what's good for me are slowly making me want to strangle him." She stood and reached out her hand. "Come on. We need to go. Or we're going to miss the photographer."

Ryder realized he shouldn't be giving himself a hard time for wanting clarification. They were embarking on a fake relationship. The normal rules of engagement did not apply.

Ryder paid the bill and they headed to the 14th Street entrance to the High Line, a former elevated train line that had been saved from demolition and converted into a public greenway a little more than a mile long with unique views of the city and lined with gardens and art. It was an oasis of calm, and one of Ryder's favorite spots to clear his head. It was particularly beautiful up there at this moment, with the sun slowly setting, casting ribbons of orange and purple across the sky. And of course, holding hands with Alex made it feel incredibly romantic. *This isn't real*, he reminded himself for what felt like the fiftieth time. He could not get sucked in by the setting, or by her. He had to stay strong and keep to his goals—preserving his relationship with Daniel, making a connection with a potential new client in Geoffrey Burnett and helping Alex through a difficult time along the way. *Keep it together. Just keep it together.*

About twenty minutes into their leisurely stroll, he felt a gentle tug on his hand. Alex was walking even slower now. Hesitating. "Everything okay?" he asked.

"Oh, yeah. Of course." Her tone told a different

story than her words. She sounded anxious. With a nod, she gestured to a small stand of bamboo and wildflowers ahead to the right. Sure enough, a man with a camera was lurking in the shadows.

Ryder instantly felt protective of Alex. He wanted to wrap her up in his arms and shield her from all of this. He knew what the press was capable of, especially when it came to her. Knowing that she was on edge made his instincts even sharper. She hated these people and she'd intentionally put herself in their path. "It's okay. It'll be okay. I promise."

"Thanks."

This wasn't his world at all, but he had to take charge or Alex wouldn't achieve her goal of a photo in the tabloids. "Honey, come here," he said, a little too loudly. "Isn't it beautiful tonight?" He led her to the railing on the west side, where there was a gap that framed a view of the Hudson River.

The water glimmered in silver and black, lit up by the lights of the city with a little extra help from the moon. They stood side by side and he carefully put his arm around her shoulders, then pulled her close. He could feel her breaths, and how shallow they were. He could only imagine what might be going through her head right now. The media had been so brutal with her. Relentless. And yet she was in the absurd position of needing to mold the narrative she knew they would pursue. He understood her need to fake it. This was about self-preservation. It was about moving on. He had his role to play, and he would not let her down.

He pulled her into an embrace, and for a moment, she rested the side of her face against his chest. He threaded his fingers through her hair, inhaled her sweet scent and kissed the top of her head. This was not an easy moment to endure. Every molecule of his body was telling him that this was right, while his brain was screaming that it was wrong. If Alex knew what was going through his head, she would have said it was black-and-white thinking. Maybe she really did have him all figured out. She certainly knew how to get to him. It would always be an exercise in restraint to be near her. This push and pull inside him would never go away. So it was time to do what they'd come here for.

As if she'd heard his silent conclusion, she raised her head and peered up into his face. Her eyes reflected so much vulnerability. It would have been the easiest thing in the world to fall for her right then and there. But he had his charge and it had nothing to do with love, even if it felt so damn real.

He cupped both sides of her face and slanted his head, then lowered his mouth until it claimed hers. The instant their skin touched, the connection had been made, and he closed his eyes and went with it, if only to put on the most convincing show possible. It wasn't a difficult task. They already knew their way around each other. It took only a second before she was pressing hard against him, making his whole body go tight as her luscious lips parted and her tongue met his. The whole experience was so raw and natural. He had to believe that no one would ever think this had been planned. Or for their sake, he hoped to hell that was true.

Alex turned her head to the other side and went back in, deeper and harder with the kiss, curling her fingers into his shoulder blades and slipping her knee between his legs. Ryder felt his body respond with a rush of blood straight to his groin. He angled his hips away from where the photographer had been standing. It wasn't going to do him any good if that got in the paper and he had to explain to Daniel why he'd gotten a raging hard-on while kissing his sister.

Slowly, he pulled his lips from hers, but not so far as to suggest that he didn't want her badly. That was an easy thing to play for the cameras. He *did* want her, even more than he had the night they slept together. "Do you think that was good?" he whispered. "Was it enough?" His heart was beating so fiercely that he was surprised he had the energy to speak. And of course, there was the complication of his erection. But he'd worry about that later. He didn't dare open his eyes, and instead simply waited for an answer.

She raked her fingers into the hair at his nape and pulled his head down, closer to her lips. "One more kiss. Just to be sure."

Three

Friday morning, Ryder zipped up his suitcase, then grabbed the suit bag holding his tux for the wedding. He was about to head out the door when his phone rang with a call from Daniel. "Hey. Is everything okay?" Ryder asked. "How have your meetings been?" Daniel was in London, meeting with a potential new client.

"Things are great. I can catch you up on it later. Work isn't the reason I'm calling, actually."

"What's up? I only have a minute. I'm supposed to pick up your sister in fifteen."

"Just tell me this kiss is fake. That's my only thing. Because it really doesn't look fake."

As much as Ryder had *not* forgotten about the

kiss, it had slipped his mind that a photo of it might hit the tabloids that morning. Or at least that had been Alex's plan. Ryder didn't know much about that world. He tried hard not to spend too much time thinking about things like that. "Did you go looking for the story?"

"No. I have an alert set up for my sister's name. With everything she's been through in the last year, I want to know about it when the tabloids are dragging her through the mud."

"I haven't seen it, but I can tell you that there's nothing between me and Alex." It bothered him a little more every time he had to insist about this, but he tried to remind himself that this was all in his control. He would simply make it so that nothing happened between him and Alex. "You trust me, don't you?"

"Of course I do. It's just…"

"What?"

"You'll have to forgive me, but seeing this picture of you kissing my sister is freaking me out. I can't help it."

It had been one thing for Daniel to state his reasons for not wanting Ryder anywhere near Alex, but it was quite another to hear that he was having such a visceral reaction to the idea. "It's fake, Daniel. Calm down. Take a breath."

"Alex is going to be so upset when she sees the headline."

Ryder winced as he let himself out of his apartment and locked the door behind him. He hated the idea of Alex getting hurt. "Do I even want to know what it says?"

"'Swept away by the trust fund tornado.' You're the one who's swept away, I guess."

Ryder groaned. "That's so unfair to Alex." *And yet, still somewhat accurate when it comes to me.*

"They're saying you're the bravest man in Manhattan."

Good God, that was even worse. He didn't consider himself brave. He was lucky that he got to kiss her at all, even if it couldn't become a habit. "I hate these people."

"Me too. You should be prepared. She's not going to be in a good mood today. There's just no way."

"Got it."

"And you're already going to a wedding, which will be triggering for her."

Ryder hoped that he was capable of handling this. He didn't do well with managing emotions. "Any suggestions?"

"Distract her whenever possible. And try to get her talking whenever you can. I know it's not your forte, but she does better when she can get these things off her chest."

Ryder drew in a deep breath as he pushed the button for the elevator. He could think of plenty of ways to distract Alex, all of which Daniel would never approve. "Got it. I need to go, but we'll catch up later?"

"Yes. Just remember our deal. No funny business with my sister."

Ryder stifled a sigh. "You have nothing to worry about. I'll talk to you later, okay?"

"Okay. Bye."

Ryder ended the call, knowing that he absolutely could not let Daniel down. Last night had called things into question, but perhaps that was merely the wake-up call he'd needed. He knew what Alex did to him, so he just had to make a point to keep things between them as platonic as possible. At least they would be sleeping in separate beds.

Downstairs in the garage, he hopped into his Bentley SUV to pick up Alex. It was an absurdly expensive car for a guy who had grown up the way he had, with very little money. In his mind, it was a reminder of how far he'd come, and how hard he'd worked. But his dad thought Ryder was punching above his weight with the fancy car and the penthouse apartment, trying to exist in a world that he didn't belong in. It was impossible to win—he either had too much or never enough. More black-and-white thinking? Maybe Alex had been right about that.

He pulled into the garage at Alex's building in the Chelsea neighborhood and sent her a text. I'm downstairs. Ready when you are.

On my way.

He put away his phone and kept an eye on the exit where she would be coming out, quickly realizing that the last time he'd been here, he'd escaped through that very door, after he and Alex had their one-night stand. His memories of that night were jumbled in his head, and he really wished it wasn't that way, but Alex was exactly that disorienting.

He remembered the beginning clearly enough. They'd run into each other at the hospital fundraiser, and she not only looked absolutely gorgeous, she also flirted and laughed and kept touching him—his hand, his arm. It didn't take long before they were in the hall outside the hotel ballroom kissing, and with Daniel nowhere near them, it had been much easier to throw caution to the wind. So, yes, he'd accepted her invitation back to her apartment. And within milliseconds of walking through her door, clothes were starting to come off. That was when it all turned to a blur in his head. Her luscious naked body, her hands and lips all over his, and him returning the favor. But after the bliss of several orgasms, when sleep threatened to take over, Ryder's conscience kicked in. He knew then that it would never, ever be enough with Alex. He would always want more. Which would never work. So he had to collect his clothes from the floor, write her an apology, ride the elevator downstairs and slink through the very doorway he was staring at right now.

Just like that, the door flew open and Alex emerged. The vision of her hit him like a bolt of lightning. He was in so much trouble. The next three days, and more important, two nights, were going to be a marathon. She was more than simply beautiful.

She was magnetic, and it was like his entire body was made of metal. Frankly, it was a miracle that he'd been able to walk away from that kiss last night. It would have been all too easy to give the tabloids far more than they ever bargained on.

He hopped out of the car and opened the tailgate to stow her luggage. "Hey. How are you?" He did his best to sound nonchalant. Like a friend, and nothing more.

She shrugged. "As good as can be expected, I suppose."

"The story in the paper?" He took her suitcase from her.

"I don't know what I expected. It's my own fault. It was my own brilliant plan. I just forgot that they could portray me however they wanted to. And boy, did they."

His heart went out to her, but it felt as though a gesture like a hug was ill-advised given his profound weakness for her. So he patted her on the shoulder instead. "Let's try to frame it positively. It did what you wanted it to do."

She managed half a smile. "I would love it if some of your optimism could rub off on me."

The word *rubbing* out of Alex's mouth only sent his brain off in several sexy directions. "Come on. I'll let you pick the music for our drive." Ryder opened Alex's door for her, then rounded to his side of the car and climbed inside. "Next stop, the Klein family estate in Connecticut."

"Next stop, wedding hell."

Ryder turned on the engine, pulled out of his parking space and had them on their way. "I don't want you to think of it that way. You must be happy that Chloe's getting married."

"Oh, I am. I love it. She and Parker are perfect for each other. I just hate the feelings that it's bringing up in me. It's one thing to work on floral arrangements or deal with brides all week long. I rarely end up attending those events. This one, I'll be in the thick of it for the whole thing."

Despite Ryder's promise to keep things with Alex as fake as could be, he wasn't going to pass up this chance to be there for her. "Look. I want you to think of me as your support system. Whatever you need from me this weekend, do not hesitate to ask."

"Really?"

"Of course. A drink. A shoulder to cry on. Whatever it is."

"Honestly, the thing I'm most dreading is time with my mom. I can already predict what she's going to say. She's going to go on and on about how it should be me who's getting married. And how if I hadn't messed up things with Henry, I would be happy right now."

The subject of Henry Quinn and Alex canceling their wedding still baffled Ryder. The day before the wedding, when he ran into Alex and he was so surprised to see she was incredibly upset about the pending nuptials, he remembered thinking that if a guy like Henry couldn't keep Alex happy, no man would ever be enough for her. Henry wasn't simply rich. He was so wealthy that he could never come close to spending his money. Henry's piles of money made more piles, every minute of every day. While he slept. While he drank his morning coffee. And it wasn't just him—generations of Quinns before him had similar wealth and power. It was the only life he knew, whereas that world of luxury and influence was still quite new to Ryder. He wasn't sure what Alex was looking for, but the bar seemed impossibly high. "I'm sure your mom won't be like that."

"You're only saying that because you have a soft spot for my family."

"I don't think that's true."

"Well, maybe not for my mom, but definitely for my dad."

"First off, I think both of your parents are great. But, yes, your dad has a special place in my heart. He gave Daniel and me the seed money to start our firm. He connected us with a lot of important people, many of whom became our first clients. And he's continued to be incredibly supportive. It's one thing to do those things for Daniel, but he didn't have to do that for me. That means a lot." Indeed, Charles Gold had done things for Ryder that his own dad never would have been in a position to do. He did not fault his father, but it did make him feel that much more indebted to the Gold family. What if Ryder had never met Daniel? He might be struggling in a small firm as a junior architect. Instead, he was co-owner of a fast-growing, immensely successful firm. Talent was important, but Ryder knew that connections were even more crucial. This wedding was the perfect example—it gave Ryder access to Geoffrey Burnett, and that all came because Daniel had plugged him into this world.

"I know my family's help has meant a lot to you," Alex said. "Believe me, I know."

Ryder steeled himself and focused on the road. He couldn't ignore the lingering subtext that he was putting his allegiance to her family ahead of anything romantic with her. But he couldn't risk it all simply because of their attraction. Alex wanted far more than Ryder would ever be able to give.

With traffic, it was more than an hour until they arrived at the tall pillars marking the entrance to the Klein estate. Ryder drove slowly down the crushed-stone driveway. All around them were centuries-old trees, rolling stretches of deep green lawn and manicured hedges. The Klein family were old money and it showed. He could feel the history and grandeur as they approached the circular drive and the house beyond, which stood strong and proud like a castle. Like many older aristocratic homes in this part of Connecticut, the structure was a clever mix of French and English design, with leaded windows, turrets and a granite foundation blanketed in ivy.

Alex's friend Taylor, willowy and blonde, emerged from the front door, along with a tall man Ryder recognized as hotelier Roman Scott. Taylor had plans to turn the estate into a boutique hotel, and Roman had come up here earlier in the summer to advise her on the process. According to Alex, the pair had undeniable chemistry, and quickly became romantically involved. Now they were apparently inseparable.

"Alex!" Taylor exclaimed when Ryder had parked the car and they climbed out. She eagerly wrapped Alex up in a hug.

Meanwhile, Roman strode over to Ryder and thrust out his hand. "Roman Scott. I've heard a lot of great things about your work. It's nice to finally put a face with the name."

Ryder shook his hand, pleased that a man as formidable as Roman Scott knew who he was. Ryder and Daniel were making waves in real estate development circles, another reason to stay laser focused on work. "Roman, it's really good to meet you, too. I know we're here for Chloe and Parker's wedding, but I'd love to talk a little shop if there's any downtime."

Roman grinned. "I think we'll be able to get away with at least a little bit of that over the weekend."

"Are you two talking about work?" Alex asked.

"You're surprised?" Taylor added with a clever arch of her eyebrows.

"Not particularly," Alex replied.

Roman slung his arm around Ryder's shoulders. "We work in the same world. Nothing wrong with forming a friendship over that."

"Let's go inside so I can show you two to your room," Taylor said.

"I'll grab our bags." Ryder clicked his fob to raise the tailgate.

"No, no, no." Taylor pulled a small walkie-talkie from her hip and spoke into it. "We need a bell-man out front for luggage pickup." She smiled as she tucked the device away. "I've got all the bells and whistles now that I'm practicing my skills with running a hotel. Now come on inside."

Alex cleared her throat and held out her hand for Ryder, reminding him that he was now, officially, her fake wedding date. He took her hand, wondering if it would ever not strike him that it fit perfectly in his. Everything about her was impossibly soft and warm. Tempting. Since he wasn't much of an actor, he supposed that if he had to fake it with someone, it was better that it was someone he was so attracted to. But it certainly didn't make the part about stopping before anything happened any easier.

Taylor and Roman led the way over to the wide stone steps and then up into the foyer, with Alex and Ryder behind them. There were people all over the place milling about. This wedding was going to be a beehive of activity.

"I'm going to check on a few things for Taylor," Roman said. "But we should grab a drink if you want, Ryder. Maybe in the main study in fifteen?"

"Sure," Ryder answered, glad he'd have something to do while Alex started dealing with the wedding.

Taylor took a kiss on the cheek from Roman, then led them up a grand spiral staircase surrounded by a bay of windows, which provided a spectacular view of the estate's entrance. At the top of the stairs were three halls and Taylor guided them to the one on the right, all the way to the end. "You two are in here," she said. "Let me know if you need anything at all."

Alex turned to her. "Thanks, hon. But you don't need to wait on us. I know you're busy with other stuff."

"Don't think twice about it. This is fun for me."

"I love seeing you and Roman together. You seem so happy." There was no mistaking the tone in Alex's voice, one of happiness but with a bittersweet edge of sadness.

"Thank you. We are. I hope you two have a great time together." She slid Ryder a glance and winked, which he took as a sign that she knew the full breadth of the situation between himself and Alex.

"Thanks, Taylor." Ryder waited for Alex to go first into their room.

She took a few steps then froze. "Huh."

Ryder followed, quickly realizing what she was surprised to see. "There's only one bed. You said there would be two."

"That's what Taylor told me." Alex turned and ducked out into the hall. "Taylor?" she called, then quickly returned to their room. "She's gone already."

Ryder wasn't sure of much, but he was absolutely certain of one thing—his plan to keep things platonic with Alex was not going to work if they were sleeping in the same bed. "Well, one of us needs to find her. I don't see how this can possibly work."

"Am I really that horrible?"

"No. You're the opposite of horrible. Which is why I intend to keep my promise to your brother, no matter what." He stuffed his hands into his pockets, unable to keep his eyes off that bed. Was it unusually small? It seemed so. All he could imagine was the things he wanted to do to Alex in that bed. Then his mind was flooded with the things Daniel would do to him if he ever found out. Bottom line, he and Alex could *not* sleep together, literally or figuratively. "Will you talk to her when you see her?"

"I will."

He hoped that this could get worked out. Otherwise, he wasn't sure what he was going to do. Sleep on the floor, most likely. His resolve was strong, but he wasn't a superhero. There was only so much of Alex's brand of temptation he could take. "I'm going to go downstairs to find Roman and find out when Geoffrey will be here. I'll see you at dinner?"

"Sure thing, Ryder," Alex said, not seeming sure of anything.

Alex watched as Ryder walked away, thinking about the many times in her life that she'd wondered what a hot guy was thinking. The trouble with Ryder was that she knew exactly what was on his mind—he was not going to allow himself to be tempted by her. The entire concept was laughable, as if she might wile him with charm that was impossible to resist. Her love life was enough evidence that she was not that woman. She also knew what was truly important to him this weekend—his work. Neither of these revelations came as a surprise. But they did come as a disappointment.

"You're just going to have to try a little harder," she muttered to herself before stepping back into their room and closing the door behind her. This might be her only chance to get another taste of Ryder. She had to up her game. As to what might happen after that, the future was entirely unclear.

She grabbed her toiletry bag and took it into the bathroom for a quick refresh, looking into the mirror and taking several deep breaths before she touched up her makeup. The sting of that morning's tabloid story was still with her. How could she have been so naive? To think that she could simply get Chloe to tip off a photographer and the press would miraculously start portraying her in a positive light? Of course they'd used the fabricated kiss and date against her, calling Ryder the bravest man in Manhattan. Of course they'd called her the trust fund tornado again. Alex had grown immune to many of the horrible things they said about her, but now they were launching insults at Ryder. Had it sealed her fate with him? Surely a guy like Ryder, intelligent, driven and highly skilled at avoiding drama, would never choose to be a part of her mess of a life. Even if she managed to fix the problems with her brother, the reality of being Alexandra Gold would still be there, ugly scars and all.

So maybe she'd convince Ryder to give her that taste this weekend, but even if she did, that would likely be the extent of it. Which meant she had to stop stressing over it. She'd do her best, then leave it to fate. For now, she really needed to concentrate on her real task for the weekend, helping Chloe with her wedding.

As if Taylor knew what she was thinking about, Alex got a text from her. Flowers were delivered. Out by the pool. Do you want to give them the once-over?

Yes. On my way. Alex rushed downstairs, finding Taylor in the kitchen, which had an extensive view overlooking the back patio and pool area. "Do you have a sec to come outside with me? I need to talk to you about something."

"Yeah. Of course," Taylor answered, leading the way outside.

Alex beelined to one of several tables situated poolside and began perusing the arrangements. The team at Flora had done an impeccable job with every arrangement, bouquet and corsage, and the delivery driver had obviously treated the flowers like the precious cargo they were.

"What's up?" Taylor asked. "You wanted to talk?"

Alex scanned the area outside to see if anyone might be listening. "One of the caterers?" she asked, nodding in the direction of a young woman with short dark hair dressed in black pants and a plain white blouse. The woman was busy folding napkins.

"Yes. I think her name is Ruby."

"I don't want to sound paranoid, but are you sure of that? She's not an undercover reporter or photographer?"

Taylor shook her head. "Alex. Please. Chloe only invited two writers and they don't get here until tomorrow. And knowing the publications they write for, I don't think they'd be caught dead wearing a caterer's uniform."

Alex sighed. She needed to stop worrying and get on with the matter at hand. "You put us in a room with one bed," she whispered to Taylor. "And Ryder's not happy about it."

Taylor's eyes went wide with surprise and she reached for Alex's arm, giving it a gentle squeeze. "You were serious about that request? I thought you were kidding."

"Why would you think that?"

"Because you've had the hots for him forever? I thought I was doing you a favor."

Alex appreciated that Taylor thought that way. Under any other circumstance, she'd be lavishing her friend with affection for perfectly cueing up two romantic nights with the guy of Alex's dreams. But Ryder had been very specific. He wanted two beds. "If he wasn't so determined for us to have a very platonic weekend, it would have been a huge favor.

Unfortunately, it's clear that his real loyalty is to my brother, and he's committed to keeping our romantic relationship fake. Unless there's a miracle of some sort, nothing will be happening between us."

Taylor grimaced. "I don't really have anywhere else to put you. Every single room is occupied. I gave the one with two beds to Chloe's teenage cousins. And I don't think I can move them because they'll just go to Chloe. They complained about me to her after they discovered I didn't have oat milk for their coffee this morning."

Alex didn't want to make any trouble for anyone, but especially not Taylor or Chloe. Ryder was just going to have to deal with sleeping in the same bed with her. Which also meant Alex would have to endure the ensuing rejection that would likely play out over the next two nights. "You know, don't worry about it. We'll figure it out. Or he can sleep in the bathtub."

Taylor shot her a questioning look. "You're kidding now, right?"

Alex shrugged. "Sorta." She decided it was time to return her focus to the wedding preparations that needed to get done. "Is there a place where I can move the flowers? We need to get these tables ready for the rehearsal dinner."

Taylor's walkie-talkie chirped. "Taylor, can you come to the service entrance? We have a delivery that isn't on the schedule," the voice crackled.

"Is that Roman?" Alex asked.

"Yes." Taylor smiled, then held up a finger before she spoke into the device. "I'll be right there."

"I love that he's so invested in the estate. In you."

Taylor grinned and got this very wistful look in her eye. If anyone had been through the wringer with men, it was her. She deserved this happiness. "He's been such a savior. He just jumped right in to help with everything. I don't know what I did to get so lucky, but that's how I feel. Very, very lucky."

Alex was genuinely happy for her friend, but still wondered if she'd ever have a love like that. She desperately wanted a shot at it with Ryder, but the likelihood of that happening was slim. "Go ahead and check on the delivery. I'll deal with the flowers."

"I can help with the flowers," said a quiet voice behind Alex as Taylor left.

She turned to see the woman in the catering uniform. "Okay. Great." She reached out her hand. "Hi. I'm Alex."

"Alexandra Gold. I know who you are," the woman replied.

Alex was a little surprised. "Because of the wedding?"

"From the tabloids and the gossip columns. You're the trust fund tornado. It would be impossible to not know who you are."

"Oh." This was an incredibly awkward start to this conversation, and Alex wasn't sure where to take it next.

"The nicknames they give you are horrible. Is it hard to handle? Or are you able to ignore it?"

Alex managed a thin smile. "They're not my favorite. That's for sure."

"Of course. You're from a rich and powerful family. So maybe you're used to being a target."

That prompted a pause from Alex. She might be notorious, but she certainly wasn't famous, and she hated that a stranger knew so much about her. "Believe me, I'm not used to any of it." She was eager to change the topic. "Any thoughts on where we can put these flowers?"

"Yes. The utility room near the butler's pantry. It's nice and cool in there, so nothing will wilt."

"Great. Sounds perfect."

Alex and Ruby began moving the floral centerpieces inside for safekeeping until the tables for dinner were all set up. They used the fridge in the garage for more delicate items like bouquets and corsages, things that they wouldn't need until tomorrow. Despite the initial awkwardness with Ruby, Alex soon found her invaluable. Frankly, she seemed to be everywhere, knew everything, and everyone, which was a great help because the catering manager was having car problems and wasn't yet on-site. When Alex needed to go over the bar setup for dinner that night, Ruby was there, taking notes for the bartender and equipped with answers about which wines and specialty cocktails they'd be serving. When Alex was frantic because she was certain that the correct linens had not been delivered, Ruby popped into another room and returned with the right ones in hand. She helped with last-minute changes to the seating plan, made sure the DJ set up in as unobtrusive a place as possible and assisted Alex as they assembled the floating lanterns that would decorate the pool for tonight and tomorrow.

"Ruby, if I could clone you, I would. You're absolutely magnificent," Alex said as she and Ruby stood and looked out at their handiwork. Round tables skirted the flagstone patio, topped with white-and-gold tablecloths, elegant place settings and the arrangements Alex had designed, complete with white magnolia blossoms and delicate cream-colored freesia. Square rice paper lanterns edged with gold ribbon gently bobbed on the surface of the pool, ready to add a soft, ambient glow when the sun began to set.

"I'm just doing my job," Ruby said shyly. "But thank you."

"I'm truly appreciative. It just feels good to get things under control. I have to tell you, I was feeling a little frantic and all over the place earlier."

"Like a tornado?"

Alex took a beat. *Tornado?* Was she seriously launching her most hated and most-used nickname at her right now? "Excuse me?"

"I'm sorry. That was a bad attempt at a joke. I was trying to be funny."

True, it wasn't exactly laughable, but Alex also

took pride in not taking herself too seriously. And although Ruby was a bit awkward, she'd been such a huge help. "Don't worry about it. I'm not offended."

"Okay, good. I wouldn't want to get into trouble. I need this job." Ruby averted her eyes.

Alex felt bad. She wondered about Ruby's lot in life. Was she scraping by? Working paycheck to paycheck? "You don't have anything to worry about, Ruby. Whenever I get a chance to speak to your boss, I'll be sure to let him or her know that you've done a wonderful job."

"Thank you, Ms. Gold. That means a lot to me. I'd better get back to work."

"Sounds good. I'll see you later."

With an hour to go until the rehearsal, Alex headed back upstairs to get dressed. When she arrived at their room, she could smell Ryder's cologne. Her heart immediately skipped a beat, but she soon realized she was all alone. One step into the bathroom and she felt the humidity in the air and saw the bath towel draped over the shower rod. He'd obviously come up to shower and dress for dinner without so much as checking in with her. Was he avoiding her? Probably. Was she going to let that get to her? Only a little. She stepped back into the bedroom and saw that he'd hung up his tuxedo in the closet, but he hadn't actually unpacked his bag, which was likely his way of holding out hope that they would eventually have the chance to move into another room, one where they had separate beds and he didn't have to be "tempted" by her. *As if.*

Knowing she couldn't worry about anyone other than herself, she changed into the dress she'd brought for tonight, a pale aqua strapless gown that was not only beautiful, but surprisingly stretchy and comfortable. She put her hair up in a bun and fixed her makeup, then headed back downstairs. She found Ryder out by the pool with Roman, Parker and Chloe. There were about a dozen other guests around, mostly family.

Alex immediately went to greet Chloe, who she still hadn't seen because she'd been off with her mom. "How's the bride?" Alex couldn't ignore the funny things her voice had done when she'd asked the question. It started with an excited squeak, but broke with *bride*. It was a loaded word for Alex. She'd been called that for an entire year before her life blew up.

Chloe, who was wearing a gorgeous silvery gray bias-cut dress, gave her a hug. "I'm just trying to not be frazzled."

"Didn't you and your mom have a spa day?"

"Yes. The spa day part was relaxing. It was my mom who undid all of that."

Alex took her friend's hand. "I'm sorry. I know exactly how stressful that can be." Memories of pre-wedding activities with her mom ran through her consciousness—the final dress fitting, manicures and facials, and lunches with family who came into town early. Alex still couldn't believe how close she'd come to getting married to the wrong guy. She also couldn't believe that more than a year later, she'd made zero progress with the one she was sure was Mr. Right. "Just remember that this is your weekend. And Ryder and I will try our best to keep your mom distracted whenever possible."

"What did you just promise I'd do?" Ryder asked.

Alex glanced over at him as he stepped closer. Dammit, he looked impossibly handsome in his dark blue suit. It was the perfect contrast to his brown eyes. His facial scruff was neat and tidy and he smelled so good that she wanted to climb inside his jacket. Although the fake date aspect of their arrangement was endlessly frustrating, Alex used it to her best advantage in this situation and took his hand and squeezed it tight. "I said that we would help Chloe by distracting her mom."

"Oh, uh, sure." He seemed surprised by the hand-holding, but quickly got with the program, kissing her on the temple, leaving behind a wonderful tingle. "We can do that." He looked over at Chloe. "Do you know when your uncle Geoffrey is set to arrive? I'm really hoping to meet him."

"He won't be here until tomorrow morning. He was supposed to come tonight, but he got held up with work stuff."

"Oh." Ryder sounded incredibly disappointed, a stark reminder of the things he cared about most.

"Do you need me to introduce you?" Chloe asked.

"That would be great," he replied.

Chloe glanced at Alex. "Actually, Alex, you've met him before. At my college graduation?"

Funny, but that had completely slipped Alex's mind. "Oh, right. I forgot about that." She turned and peered up at Ryder. "If Chloe's not around, I'm sure I can make the introduction."

"Sorry, guys," Chloe said. "Parker wants me to spend some time with his dad." With a nod, she gestured to the other side of the pool area, where Parker was waving her over.

"No problem. We'll see you up in the clearing for the rehearsal." The ceremony tomorrow was set to take place in a picturesque spot on the hill along one side of the property that was surrounded by woods on three sides and provided a stunning view down to Long Island Sound.

"Sounds good." With that, Chloe was off to catch up with Parker.

"I saw that you didn't unpack your things upstairs," Alex said. "Unfortunately, Taylor doesn't have anywhere else to put us."

"Oh. Okay."

"I'm sorry."

"Don't apologize, Alex. It's not your fault. It's not anyone's fault."

She leaned closer to him. "I wouldn't want you to think I'm unfairly trying to tempt you."

He looked down at her, their gazes connecting.

"If you didn't want to tempt me, you wouldn't be wearing that dress."

A smile bloomed on her face. When he said things like that, it only made her want him more. As far as she was concerned, it should be impossible for him to deny their chemistry. Their connection. It was real and palpable and so worth giving in to. Maybe she simply needed to try harder. Wear him down. Make him want her. She smoothed her hand over his lapel. "If I was really going to tempt you, Ryder, I wouldn't be wearing anything at all."

Four

The wedding rehearsal went off without a hitch. Chloe and Parker, along with Alex and Ryder, Taylor and Roman, and Chloe's parents stood in the clearing, overlooking Long Island Sound as they went through the choreography of the ceremony with the officiant. A warm late-summer breeze swept through the area and Alex had tried to focus on getting through it, rather than more memories of the preparations for the wedding that never happened.

The dinner that followed was also perfect. The food, the wine and flowers were all flawless. Not a single thing went wrong. Ruby checked in with Alex once, just to reassure her that all was good, as she'd had to take over because the catering manager never arrived. All in all, Alex couldn't have asked for anything more. One more hurdle was behind her, and Chloe was one step closer to the start of her new life with Parker. So why was Alex feeling like things weren't quite right?

The question rang loudly in her head as Parker and Chloe were the first couple out on the dance floor, wrapped up in each other's arms, gazing into each other's eyes. Ryder was a few feet away from Alex, quietly chatting with Roman. He looked as though he didn't have a worry in the world, laughing and smiling and occasionally taking a sip of his drink. He was so close, and her longing for him was so present in her body, it was like the blood that coursed through her veins. She couldn't have him. He wasn't hers. Even though they could be perfect together. Yes, she could take two or three steps to be at his side. She could take his hand. She might even be able to persuade him to kiss her on the cheek or the top of her head, all to keep up the appearance that they were a couple. But as good as those things would feel, every time they happened, the line between fantasy and reality blurred a little more, and Alex felt that much more lost. Not that she had any choice in the matter. They'd sold the idea that they were together. And they had to keep that up.

As soon as that first song ended, Chloe turned and pointed at Taylor, then waved her up onto the dance floor. Taylor grabbed Roman's hand and followed the directive. Alex was Chloe's next target, as she mouthed, *Get up here.*

Alex looked at Ryder. "Care to dance?" She hated that she had to ask, but he showed no sign of taking initiative.

"You don't sound superenthused."

I would be if I thought it could lead to anything. I would be if every minute of this evening wasn't another reminder of everything that's wrong with my life. She reached for his hand. "No, really. I'm thrilled." She didn't wait for more discussion on the topic, marching across the patio as he tagged along so they could join the other couples already dancing. When they arrived, she turned to him and put her available hand on his shoulder, but she couldn't look him in the eye. It was only going to piss her off.

Ryder settled his hand at her waist. That one touch was enough to make her silently groan in pleasure. Why was she so addicted to him? Why did he have to have such control over her? And would she ever be able to get past this? That was the biggest question before her.

He swayed them back and forth to a song that was desperately romantic, and ideal for a rehearsal dinner party, but distinctly annoying for Alex. "I have a feeling something's wrong," he said.

She shook her head, still afraid to make eye contact with him. "I'm fine."

"Alex…" He lowered his head, trying to catch her attention. "What's going on?"

She turned away. "Stop it."

"Stop what?"

"Stop being cute and concerned."

He cleared his throat. "So you'd be happier if I was ugly and aloof? Because I'm willing to do whatever it takes to get you out of this sour mood."

"I'm not in a sour mood. I'm just wrestling with a few things. That's all."

He slid his hand to the center of her back and pulled her a little closer. "I have a feeling I know what you're talking about. It's no surprise that this weekend is hard for you. Is there anything I can do?"

She drew in a deep breath through her nose. She didn't want to get into it. She might start crying, or worse, she might completely fall apart, and she didn't want to do that to Chloe. "Just dance with me. That's all." She closed her eyes and drank in his smell, choosing to think of it as pure comfort, like a warm blanket. Nothing else. Certainly not anything sexual.

"I can do that."

"Good." She swayed back and forth in his arms, willing her shoulders to loosen. Unfortunately, the more she managed to relax, the more her body chose to remind her who she was dancing with. A gentle wave of warmth started in her belly and rolled down past her hips and up along her torso. Meanwhile, the two sides of her brain were starting to argue.

You could kiss him and he wouldn't be able to do or say anything.

Hey, what about consent? Holding hands is one thing, but you can't take advantage of him like that.

Luckily, the song ended, which let her set aside her conflicting thoughts. "Okay. I think we're good. One song is probably enough to convince everyone."

Ryder didn't let go. Instead, he pulled her even closer, so abruptly that it forced a sharp breath from her lips. "I don't want to let you go right now," he said. "Something is going on with you and I want you to tell me what it is. Be specific. Get it off your chest. I think you'll feel better."

"I'm positive that you don't want to hear any of it. Plus, I don't want to talk about it here. On the dance floor." Finally, she dared to look up into his face. His eyes were so kind it made it hard to breathe.

"Then we'll talk about it upstairs."

"We can't leave the party."

"Why not? Aren't you done with your duties for the day?"

"Yes. But wouldn't it be rude?"

He shrugged and pulled her closer again. "You've got to be tired, and tomorrow is going to be a hard day. I think it would be okay for you to duck out. Plus, everyone thinks we're hot for each other. Nobody could blame us for wanting to be alone."

The truth was that Alex was exhausted, and she had a headache brewing. So maybe he was right. Perhaps a bit of sleep was all she needed to pull herself together. "Okay."

"Okay?"

She reared back her head. "Okay. Let's get out of here."

"I think it's the best decision."

Alex wandered over to Chloe and Parker, giving them both a hug and explaining that she was getting a headache and needed to catch some shut-eye. They both seemed understanding, although Chloe definitely delivered a questioning glance that seemed to ask whether Alex and Ryder were stealing away for another reason. If only Alex could tell her friend that no, they were not.

Upstairs, Alex kicked off her shoes the instant they were in their room. "Thanks for convincing me it was time to leave."

"It's fine. But now you have to tell me what's wrong."

She turned back to him. "You're acting so weird, Ryder. It's not like you to ask someone to delve into their feelings."

He rolled his arms out of his suit jacket. "I know, but I promised your brother. He said you'd be happier if you had a chance to get things off your chest."

Alex couldn't help it—she laughed. "Of course. That makes sense. Daniel is behind this."

"That's not entirely fair. I'm still the person who's asking. It does make me sad to see you unhappy, Alex."

"I'm fine."

He took a step closer. Then another. "No. You're not."

"I'm mostly fine. Is that good enough?"

He shook his head and the next thing she knew, he'd pulled her into a hug. "It's the wedding, isn't it? You're happy for Chloe, but it's still hard to see her move forward in this way. You saw yourself doing this and it didn't turn out the way you wanted it to."

For someone who was supposedly not good with feelings, he'd hit the nail right on the head. Of course he'd forgotten one part—that she wanted him and her desire was showing no signs of going anywhere. "Stop flirting with me, Ryder. Seriously." The ache for him was immense. Unbearable. He released her from his embrace, but took her hand. It felt like sheer torture. She couldn't take another minute of his comfort and consolation.

"I'm not. I'm being nice."

"No. You're making me want to kiss you. You're making me glad that there's only one bed. And I know that's not how you feel. You wish there were two. You wish we were in separate rooms. Different buildings."

"I only feel that way because I care about you, your brother and your family."

"Right. I know." She was so tired of that reason, but she knew that he wasn't using it as an excuse. It was very real to him.

"I'm serious."

"I know you are. Believe me, if anyone grasps how serious you are, it's me."

"So I think that if you don't want to talk about things, then we should both get some sleep, on our separate sides of the bed, and get you through tomorrow. Because I know it isn't going to be easy for you. On several levels."

She felt about as defeated as she'd ever felt. But again he was right. Sleep was a good idea. She'd feel better in the morning. "Okay."

"You want the bathroom?"

"I'm going to take a while. You go first."

Ryder grabbed some things from his suitcase and disappeared into the bathroom. Alex decided to change into her pajamas, thinking that either she'd have complete privacy or Ryder would accidentally see her naked and possibly change his mind. But as she went through her things, she remembered that she'd optimistically only brought a nightgown. A sexy nightgown. The kind not meant for much sleeping. The sort of lingerie that was for taking off. The only problem was she didn't have anything else to wear to bed. It was either this, one of the gowns she'd brought or nothing. So she put it on. If he was going to torment her with his presence, she'd do the same to him.

She went to the bathroom door and knocked. "Ryder? Almost done?"

"Yeah. Two secs."

"Okay." She looked down at herself, second-guessing whether this was a good idea. Or fair to him. He'd been clear about his intentions. She wouldn't be a very good friend if she actually tried to seduce him right now. "Hey, Ryder? Do you have a T-shirt I can borrow to sleep in?"

"Why? Did you forget your pajamas?"

She wrapped her arms around her middle. "Let's just say that I don't think you'll be happy with the ones I'm wearing."

Ryder stood staring at the bathroom door, confused, as he wiped toothpaste from the corner of his mouth with the hand towel. "Why would I be unhappy with your pajamas?"

"What I'm wearing just isn't great for our situation, okay?"

"Our situation?" he muttered to himself. "I don't understand." He was tired of playing these guessing games, so he opened the door. It was a big mistake. Huge.

There before him stood Alex, wearing a mindblowing silky black nightgown that skimmed over her tempting curves. It left very little to the imagination, and unfortunately for him, he'd seen the rest of her, so it didn't take much of a leap at all to fill in the parts that were covered by that impossibly thin garment. He didn't want to be a good guy anymore. He wanted to be a bad man. Very bad. He wanted to take the set of rules he'd given himself, stomp them with his shoe and grind them into nothing. He wanted to scoop Alex up into his arms, lay her down on that bed and peel the nightgown off her. He imagined his hands all over her sumptuous body, his mouth on her breasts and his fingers in her hair. And then he imagined himself inside her, bringing her to her peak and having her moan in ecstasy into his ear. They were all alone. No one had to know a thing. For that matter, nearly everyone at this wedding thought of them as a couple. It would only add to the illusion if there were a few sex noises coming from their room.

"See what I mean?" She looked down at herself, drawing attention to her cleavage. Then she pirouetted, which only made things worse, as the hem swished higher up her legs and kicked up a waft of her heavenly smell.

Grabbing the door frame, he steadied himself. "Wow. Uh. Okay. Yeah."

She narrowed her sights on him and cocked her head to the side. "Unless you're having second thoughts." She took a step closer and her eyes shifted a shade darker.

He swallowed hard. If only she knew that he was having third thoughts. And fourth. He had too many things running through his head. Good and bad. Obligations and promises. And at the center of it all was this beautiful, amazing woman who he was not meant to have. "We've been through this, Alex. I made a promise and I intend to keep it."

"Right. You're Mr. Good Guy."

He hated this feeling that it was his job to be the sensible one. His entire life was about responsibility and being judicious. "Let me get you a T-shirt, okay? Then we'll both be more comfortable and we can get some sleep." He trudged over to his suitcase and sifted through the contents until he found a shirt he'd brought for his run tomorrow morning.

"Of course." She took the garment from his hand. "It's a shirt for the MIT School of Architecture."

"Is there a problem? It's my alma mater."

"And it's where you met my brother. Your history with him is this presence that simply won't go away."

He shrugged. "Sorry. It's what I have to offer."

"It's fine. I'll be back in a minute." She floated past him and into the bathroom, but she didn't close the door all the way. She left it cracked, which was the perfect illustration of their dynamic. He could try hard to put up boundaries, but he had the distinct impression that she wasn't going to give them much respect.

Ryder walked around to the far side of the bed, pulled back the comforter and climbed in, tugging the covers up under his arms. He closed his eyes, leaving him with the sound of running water in the sink and Alex milling about in the bathroom. Eventually, there was a click and even through his closed eyelids, he could see that the room had fallen into total darkness. A moment later, she was in the bed next to him. Despite his need for sleep, all five of his senses were on high alert and they were all clued in on her.

"What time do we need to get up?" he asked.

"Breakfast is at nine. We should be at that. It's just a buffet, and the caterer should have everything under control, but I should probably get down there by eight thirty just to make sure it's all running according to plan."

He admired how she was so devoted to giving Chloe the perfect wedding weekend, especially given her history with nuptials. "I'm sorry you have to do all of this. I'm sure it's hard for you to be in the thick of it and not think about your own wedding."

"Thanks."

"It's okay to tell me you don't want to talk about it, but I do genuinely worry about you."

She blew out an exasperated breath. "And I appreciate it. I do appreciate that you're taking the time to think about how I feel in all of this. It's not a ton of fun, but I love Chloe and she's always been there for me. This is what friends do, right? We do the hard thing so we can show them how much they mean to us."

Ryder had to laugh quietly. "Yeah. I think you know that I'm more than familiar with that concept."

"Oh, God. Of course. Sorry." She shifted in the bed, rolling to her side. "You feel the same way about Daniel. That was sort of staring me in the face, wasn't it?" Her voice drifted straight into his ear. She was closer now.

"Hopefully that helps you see where I'm coming from."

She exhaled just loud enough for him to hear it. "It does."

There was one thing Ryder still didn't understand about her, and he was eager to put the pieces of this particular puzzle together. And even though she'd been hesitant to talk even fifteen minutes ago, here in the dark and the quiet, this might be his best chance to have an honest conversation with her about it. "What exactly happened? When you canceled the wedding? I saw you right before then and we talked, but honestly, I thought you were just stressed and that you'd needed to get rid of some of that burden so that you could go forward with it all. Next thing I knew, you'd called it off." He'd worried many times that he'd said the wrong thing to her that day and managed to point her in the wrong direction. But all he'd said was that she needed to follow her heart, advice which he'd assumed would lead her to Henry, her fiancé.

"Do you know why Henry and I got engaged in the first place?"

He opened his eyes, confused by the question, and rolled to his side to face her. He couldn't see every stunning detail of her face, but he could see her eyes in the darkness. She too was wide-awake. "Because you were in love?"

"No. We got engaged because he asked."

"I don't understand."

"You were there that night. My birthday."

"Of course. You invited me. Along with three hundred other people."

"That was all my mom's doing. Aside from my sweet sixteen, I've never had such a humungous birthday party. I mean, I was turning twenty-eight. Who has a giant party for that?"

"Did she know that Henry was going to propose?"

"She did. He'd gone to my parents ahead of time to ask for their blessing. I'm sure my mom was probably half out of her mind when he asked. She's obsessed with social standing and Henry's family is about as high on the ladder as you can get."

Ryder was well aware of Henry Quinn's stature when it came to wealth and power. "Do you really think she's obsessed with it? Your mom has always seemed pretty down-to-earth to me."

Alex laughed. Despite the serious nature of their conversation, it made his heart lighter, and his whole body warm. "Are you kidding me?"

"No. I'm being serious."

"Then you haven't been around my mom at her worst." She sighed. "I mean, I get it. She's an elite wedding planner and she runs in these very exclusive circles because of it, but there's always this feeling that she's an outsider. Or at least that's what she thinks. That she doesn't truly belong. And I think we all want to belong."

"Why would she be an outsider? I don't want to be crass about it, but your family is very well off. And on top of all of that, your mom is highly sought after for her talents and your dad is greatly respected in his field." Alex and Daniel's dad, Charles, was a mover and shaker in the biotech world. He'd started and more importantly, sold, several companies and made billions.

"Oh, but we're *new* money. Not old money. Even in the world of the rich, there's a stigma about where your wealth comes from. That's something I didn't learn until I went to the Baldwell School and met Taylor and Chloe. They both come from old money. Not me."

Ryder had to wonder if that was part of the reason why Alex's family had always been so warm and welcoming to him. He didn't know what they were like before Charles had made his first billion, but perhaps their generosity was because they weren't far removed from humbler beginnings. Of course, Ryder's background was beyond humble. It was blue-collar, paycheck to paycheck, through and through. "So your mom planned this big birthday party, knowing Henry was going to propose at it?"

"Yes. And I think she knew that there was no way I could tell him no. With all of those people staring at us and waiting for me to say yes."

Ryder had never thought about it in that way. A big, public proposal seemed like the ultimate romantic gesture. Not Ryder's style at all, but he assumed Henry had asked in that manner because he was absolutely certain she would say yes. "Plus, there was the ring. I don't know how you were supposed to say no to that thing. I probably would've said yes to Henry Quinn if he'd offered me a diamond that big."

Alex reached out and grabbed Ryder's arm, sending another pleasing wave of warmth through his body. "Yes. Oh, my God. It was ridiculous, honestly. I felt so self-conscious wearing it. Who wears a ten-carat diamond? Not me. It's just not my thing. It was the perfect symbol of how poorly matched we were."

"If you weren't right for each other, why did you stay with him?"

"It's a pretty ridiculous story, really. You know, we met at a mutual friend's wedding. Daniel introduced us, actually. And we sort of hit it off, I guess, although to be honest, I thought he was a little self-important. But we got drunk that night and slept together. That was the start of it."

Ryder quietly cleared his throat, not wanting to think about Henry and Alex hooking up. "Okay."

"And I just assumed that it would be a one-time thing. But then the next day, he invited me on a trip to Abu Dhabi on his private plane, and things just kind of got more outlandish from there. It was exciting at first, and I liked him okay, but I also figured that he would eventually grow tired of me. To my great surprise, he didn't."

"Alex. Why would you think that he would grow tired of you? That's a terrible thing to think about yourself."

"I don't know. Because I don't care about the things that he cares about? Things like stock portfolios and meeting famous people and jet-setting. It's not really my scene. It's fun for a little while, but then you realize how empty it all is, and there's only so much champagne a person can drink. I was think-ing, just let me get back to work. I'd rather do some-thing constructive. Not sit around and spend money."

Ryder smiled to himself. As much reason as Alex had to be as superfluous as she wanted, she was ul-timately a very grounded person. He never would have said a thing to her at the time, but the pairing of Henry and her had struck him as odd. He'd as-sumed it meant that he didn't know Alex as well as he thought he did. It was nice to be reassured that he did know her. The *real* her. "It sounds like you were riding on a runaway train."

"That's exactly what happened. And my mom wasn't being nefarious when she helped plan the party. She really thought I was in love. That's how good of a show I was putting on. And of course, as soon as the engagement happened, she was off to the races with planning the wedding. I felt like I was in a pressure cooker the whole time. Every day closer to the wedding day was a little more pressure. A lit-tle more heat."

"Until finally you couldn't take it anymore and you exploded."

She was still holding on to his arm, and she rubbed her thumb back and forth across his skin. "I'm sorry. That was the day we saw each other. I feel bad that you had to be there for that. I com-pletely fell apart."

"Don't apologize. I'm not great with feelings and emotions, but I'm glad that I could be there to listen."

She was quiet for a moment, then she let go of him. "You gave me great advice. You told me to follow my heart. Up until then, I hadn't been doing that. I'd been listening to what everyone else wanted me to do."

"That's pretty standard advice, isn't it? I didn't coin the term or anything."

"It's not exactly groundbreaking, but you'd be surprised that no one had said that to me before then. I guess you sort of shook me awake that day. And you helped me not make what would have been the biggest mistake of my life. So thank you."

"I can't take much credit. You still had to make the tough decision. There's no way that was easy."

"It definitely was not."

"I'm sorry that it thrust you into this situation you didn't want to be in. Stuck bringing a fake date to your friend's wedding, just so you could keep yourself out of the tabloids."

"You know what, Ryder?"

"What?"

"If I had to have a fake date, I'm glad it could be with you."

Ryder held his breath, feeling as thought he was right back to where he'd been before they'd gone to bed. When she was wearing that mind-blowing nightgown and he was so close to breaking his promise to Daniel. She was wearing something decidedly more modest now, but it didn't mean his desire to have her was any less. If anything, it was more powerful now. His assumptions about Alex's relationship with Henry had been all wrong. She was the exact sort of woman who could be perfect for him.

If only she wasn't his best friend's sister.

Five

Alex's eyes popped open when she woke to the sound of spraying water. She bolted upright in bed and her thoughts flew to Ryder. He was in the shower. Her first instinct was to hope that she'd be superlucky and Ryder would have left the door open. An invitation, perhaps? *Come and join me for some morning fun.* Alas, when she looked, the answer was no. The door was as shut as could be. Her heart sank and she slumped back against her pillow, then rolled to her side, eyeing the sliver of bathroom light beaming out from under the door. Somewhere on the other side, Ryder was naked. Here on this side, Alex was nothing but frustrated. She'd spent an entire night in the same bed with him, drifting in and out of sleep as he distracted her with the shockingly sexy way he breathed while sleeping. Of course, he'd managed to go the whole night without so much as grazing her leg with his foot or her arm with his hand. So close…and yet, so far.

The universe was torturing and tormenting her. He'd been so kind to her yesterday, and she'd loved being able to let down her guard last night and tell him the story of what happened with Henry. Only Taylor and Chloe knew the truth of the engagement party, but absolutely no one knew that Ryder had been the real reason she'd had the nerve to call off the wedding. She'd considered making the confession to him last night, but it felt far too monumental. They had another night to spend together in this bed. Now was not a time for dropping truth bombs that would only lead to awkwardness.

She reached over to the nightstand and yanked the charger cord from her phone, but the instant the screen lit up and she saw a long list of messages, she sensed something was wrong. Her first thought was the wedding. But it wasn't that. It was something far worse. Little Black Book had gone after her.

"What the hell?" She sat back up in bed and flicked through the texts from friends, including Taylor. After reading several messages that said things like, I'm so sorry and Someone needs to stop them, she decided to look for herself. But she wasn't truly prepared for what was waiting for her when she pulled up the social media site. The title of the post made her sick. "Revisiting the Trust Fund Tornado." It went on to recap Alex's canceled wedding, and the flurry of tabloid stories that followed, but then ended it with a bit about how she was apparently attempting to lure another man into her trap. And not just any man—Ryder. More waves of nausea hit her as she saw the final image in the carousel. It was of her and Ryder dancing at the rehearsal dinner, which had only thirty-two guests. There was only one conclusion to make. Either someone at this wedding was Little Black Book or they were feeding info to them. Both thoughts scared her.

Alex hopped out of bed and rushed to the bathroom, pounding on the door. "Ryder. We have an emergency. Can you come out here?"

"Are you hurt?"

"Mentally, yes. Physically, no."

"Okay. Hold on." A few seconds later, the door opened and Ryder was standing there clutching a towel around his waist. Beads of water dotted his shoulders and his hair was dripping with moisture. "What is it?"

Alex had a sudden urge to forget what she'd just seen on her phone so she could flatten Ryder with a kiss and a quick tug of that towel from his waist. But no. This was not the time for that. "Look." She thrust the phone in Ryder's face, trying to ignore just how badly she wanted his towel to simply be smaller. Damn Taylor and her generous bath linens.

"Wow. Are you okay?" he asked with the familiar tone he'd taken last night, the one laden with pity and that apparently made him determined to not sleep with her.

"No. And no."

"I'm sorry. It's not fair the way you've been treated."

"Thanks. It's just sort of my lot in life for the moment, I suppose." She sighed if only to let off a little steam. "Unfortunately, I don't think the post is the worst part of it. This picture is from yesterday. Either Little Black Book is in the house right now, or they're getting info from a guest."

"Wow. Parker is going to freak out. It's all he wanted to talk about yesterday, and now this?"

"Seriously. It's his wedding day. Chloe won't be happy either. I need to talk to her right away."

He nodded furiously. "I should probably talk to Parker. You go ahead and take the bathroom. I'm sure you need to get ready." He opened the door farther to let her in, then turned to squeeze past her.

His passing bare chest was sheer torture for Alex. Despite the utter chaos of her predicament, she still wanted him so bad she could taste it. Taste *him*. She turned back as he walked away, watching his perfect butt all wrapped up in a towel. One more sigh for good measure, then she closed the door. There was only so much torment she could take in one day. It wasn't even 8:00 a.m.

After cleaning up, and putting on a sundress and some sandals, she rushed downstairs to find Chloe, who was in the kitchen with her mom, Eliza, and

the one person Alex wasn't prepared to see yet—
her own mother.

"Mom," Alex said. "When did you and Dad get
here?"

Alex's mother whipped around. Her dark hair,
a near match for Alex's, was up in a high ponytail,
which really brought out her mother's high cheek-
bones. "Alexandra." She wagged her phone in the
air. "Have you seen what they're saying about you
on the internet? I would really like it if you could
stay out of the tabloids."

"Alex, I'm so sorry," Chloe said.

"Me too," Chloe's mom, Eliza, added. "It's terrible."

Alex tried very hard not to cringe. She also tried
very hard to ignore the fact that her mom's greeting
was one of shock and horror, rather than empathy.
"Yes. I've seen it all." She gave her mother a hug.
"It's nice to see you, too, Mom."

"Your dad doesn't know about this yet, thank
goodness," her mother said. "And I had to find out
about you and Ryder from the papers the other day?
Why do I always have to be the last person to find
out these things?"

Oops. Alex hadn't thought far enough ahead to
contemplate the idea that her mom would ask about
this. She pulled her aside into a corner of the kitchen.
"It's platonic. We're just friends. Chloe invited a few
select writers because they're people she works with
off and on, and I thought I could give myself a bit
of an image makeover if they thought I had a date."

"Hmm." Her mom shook her head, seeming doubtful. "Probably for the best. He's a great guy, but I'm not sure he's right for you anyway. You need someone dependable. Someone who will stick around. He never gets serious about any woman. Ever. It's not hard to see how that might be a bit of a habit for him."

"Have you been talking to Daniel? Because that last part sounds like it's straight out of his mouth." Wow, her mother was really batting a thousand today. And as much as Alex did love her mom, she couldn't stand to hear a single disparaging thing about Ryder. "He's a great guy, full stop. No need to say a single thing after that."

"It's just a shame that you can't sort out this part of your life, Alexandra. You could have had the fairytale happy ending and you threw it all away. You should be married right now. And pregnant."

Alex held up a finger to stop this line of speculative thinking, especially since her mother was so willing to say the uncomfortable part out loud. "Mom. We've been through this one hundred times. I didn't love Henry. So it's better that we aren't married and it's certainly better that there were no children involved. End of story. Next subject, please."

"Everything okay?" From behind her, Ryder put his hands on Alex's shoulders.

"Oh, hey." Alex's heart broke out into a full sprint, and not only because he was touching her. Had he heard the things that had just been said about him? She really hoped not.

"Hi, Mrs. Gold. Just saw your hubby. I'm so glad you're here," Ryder said.

"Hello, Ryder, you handsome man." Alex's mom grinned, adopting a pleasantry that made Alex so deeply uncomfortable. Mere seconds ago, she'd insisted Ryder wasn't right for her. She then turned to Parker, who had come into the room after Ryder. "And you must be the man who won dear Chloe's heart." She gave him the visual once-over, then slid Alex a look that seemed to underscore the sentiment that she could've had a man like Parker if she hadn't messed it up.

"Parker," Alex said. "This is my mom, Brigitte Gold."

"Mrs. Gold, it's nice to meet you. Thanks for coming." Parker strode across the room to Chloe's side. "While so many of you are here, we need to talk about Little Black Book." He nodded in Alex's direction. "They went after Alex this morning, but it was obvious from the post that someone at this wedding supplied them with the photos. Or even worse, that the person behind Little Black Book is here at the house right now."

"I really didn't want our wedding to be about this." Deep creases formed on Chloe's forehead. She'd long been annoyed by Parker's obsession with Little Black Book, but his history with the social media account was complicated. He was a sports agent and his star client had been Little Black Book's first target.

"Me neither, but here we are. We can't ignore it or wish it away." Parker kissed her temple.

"It's pretty terrible timing," Ryder said. "But I have to agree with Parker. We need to figure out who's behind this. I hate seeing them target Alex."

Alex smiled. At least someone had come to her defense. "Is Ruby around? She knows everyone on the catering staff. She's totally on top of things. I think she might be able to help us figure this out." Alex's brain was apparently working several seconds behind her mouth. As she heard her own words, her thoughts began lining up in a different way. She stepped closer to Chloe and whispered, "Unless. Do you think there's any chance it's Ruby?"

Chloe dropped her chin and stuck out her lower lip. "She's so nice. And competent. She helped me with all sorts of stuff yesterday. Does that make sense?"

"I know it sounds completely out there, but she made a comment yesterday about me being the trust fund tornado. And of the many horrible nicknames I've been given, isn't it a little coincidental that she chose that one, especially since that's what Little Black Book used?"

"It's also what the New York tabloids used the other day," her mother pointed out. "Maybe it's simply fresh in people's minds."

Alex didn't feel as though that deserved a direct response. Her mother was right, but it also felt like another chance for her to rub salt in Alex's wound. "I'd just like to talk to Ruby. I think she can help us get to the bottom of this."

"Maybe Taylor knows where she is?" Chloe asked, sounding distressed.

Taylor popped into the room. "Did I hear my name?"

"We're trying to figure out this Little Black Book situation and are wondering where Ruby from the catering team is," Alex answered.

"Not here," Taylor said, looking concerned. "She's over an hour late and I heard from the catering manager that Ruby's number is out of service."

"No way," Parker blurted. "The exact same thing happened to Chloe and me when we were in Miami and Little Black Book threatened us. We tried to call after they sent us a text, and the number was out of service."

"But doesn't that happen all the time?" Chloe asked. "This all feels like we're grasping at straws, when I'd rather be thinking about our wedding. I don't want to let this ruin everything."

Alex had to agree, although she was definitely going to spend some of her day hunting for Ruby. "Chloe's right. Let's stay focused on the big day."

Ryder was doing his best to keep up, but things at this wedding were moving incredibly fast and in directions no one could have predicted. By early afternoon, there was no sign of Ruby. Alex, with her amazing skills of persuasion, was able to get the catering manager to divulge that they'd never done a background check on Ruby, and she'd only been working for them for two days when she was assigned to work Chloe and Parker's wedding. Everyone now seemed convinced that Ruby either was Little Black Book or was supplying the social media account with their intel. But why? And why go after Alex? She hadn't done anything to provoke an attack like this.

Of course, Ryder had other concerns as well. Geoffrey Burnett had arrived at the house that morning, soon after Ruby became the biggest subject of conversation. Ryder never had his chance to be introduced to him. Geoffrey turned around and went golfing with his wife immediately after they had their things brought to their room. The window of opportunity was narrowing. The wedding guests would all be departing tomorrow and so much of the reason Ryder had come to this wedding would be leaving as well.

And now Daniel was texting him about it. At the airport to fly home from London. How are things with Geoffrey?

Ryder was sitting on the bed in the room he was sharing with Alex. He was already dressed in his tux for the ceremony and was waiting for Alex to finish up in the bathroom. Haven't met him yet. I'm sure I'll see him tonight.

What have you been doing this whole time?

Waiting for Geoffrey to show up. Of course, that wasn't exactly true.

We really need this. It could be a game changer.

I want this as much as you do. He hated the way Daniel sometimes talked down to him. As if Ryder didn't fully comprehend the magnitude of landing a client like Geoffrey. Of course it was important. They did nothing but strive to take their firm to greater heights, a goal equally shared by them both.

Alex okay? Saw Little Black Book. Not in the mood to ask her about it.

Ryder loved Daniel like a brother, but this made his blood simmer. Didn't Alex deserve Daniel's concern over what had happened? She did. She's great. I'm taking care of her. As soon as Ryder hit Send, he wondered if Daniel might take that the wrong way.

Taking care of her? What does that mean?

There it was. He'd definitely taken it the wrong way. I'm treating her the way you would want me to. Okay?

As long as there's nothing else.

Ryder grumbled at his phone. His best friend and business partner didn't fully trust him. There was something distinctly wrong about that. Nothing else. He hit Send, put his phone on mute and tucked it in his jacket pocket just as Alex opened the bathroom door and squeezed her face through a narrow opening.

"Can you help me with my zipper?" she asked sheepishly. "I swear this isn't a ploy. I legitimately can't reach back there and pull it up."

Ryder had to laugh as he got up from the bed. Somehow, he and Alex had reached a happy medium, where they acknowledged the sexual tension between them and were living with it. "I know it's not a ploy." He stepped into the bathroom as she turned her back to him. This was a view he wasn't entirely prepared for—the stretch of her bare skin starting at her nape and leading all the way down to the top of her lacy black panties, all of it framed by an emerald green gown. He cleared his throat and went in for the job he'd promised to do, grasping the bottom of the zipper with one hand while using the other to draw it up. But what he really wanted was to touch her. Kiss her. "All good?"

She looked back at him over her shoulder, flashing her stunning eyes. "Yep. Thank you."

He leaned against the door frame, mostly because the events of the last minute made it difficult to stand. "Um, I'm no expert on women's clothing, but don't you wear a bra with a dress like that?"

She turned and that was when he saw the deep plunge of the neckline. The pleasing curve of her breasts was right there, just like last night when she'd showed up at this very bathroom door in that maddening nightgown. Alex had such a luscious figure and he knew firsthand how incredible it was to touch every inch of her. "It doesn't really work with this one. And most couture gowns are engineered to hold things in place."

"Ah. Good." He nodded, trying hard to not think about the many things she possessed which required being kept in place. "Are we ready to head down?"

"I am."

He hesitated, the text from Daniel still on his mind. Someone needed to stick up for Alex. Someone had to make sure she was okay. "Hey, before we go, I want to tell you that I think you're doing an amazing job. The way you've handled everything. Yesterday. Today. This whole weekend." He stepped aside as she breezed past him to tuck a few things into a small handbag. "It's impressive. Between navigating everything with Little Black Book, and helping Chloe and Taylor and standing up to your mom. I don't know how you handle every bit of adversity."

She reached out for his arm. Even through the fabric of his jacket, her warmth poured into him. "You heard my mom?"

"The whole thing." In truth, the things Alex's mom had said about him never getting serious with a woman still stung. It wasn't that he planned to never settle down. He was simply focused on his career. He'd worked too hard and accomplished too much to let up now. Plus, it was out of respect for Alex's family and everything they'd done for him that Ryder was so intent on maximizing the success of Gold and Carson.

"I'm so sorry she was talking about you. She says things without thinking about it."

"That's not what I care about. I care that she was giving you a hard time about Henry and that you stood up to her. I'm sure that wasn't easy, especially considering how invested she was in you getting married."

She blew out a breath through her nose. "You helped me with that. Talking about it last night made it all a little clearer in my head, I guess because you agreed that I'd done the right thing."

He stood a little straighter. It filled him with pride to know that he'd helped her since she was so ready and willing to do the same for others. "You amaze me, Alex. Really. Truly."

She cocked her head to one side and arched an eyebrow at him in suspicion. "You're flirting with me again."

He smiled and heat rushed to his cheeks. She had such a way about her. She could always get to him. "I'm not. I swear."

She pressed a fingertip against the center of his chest. "I hate to break it to you, but your mere existence is like flirting to me."

"That can't possibly be true. Be serious."

"I've never been more serious about anything in my life." Her single finger on his chest became all five, and then it was her palm that was pressing in on him, right where his heart was. Could she feel the thump of his pulse? Did she know how nervous she could make him? "But you've been clear that Daniel's wishes take precedence. So I guess I'm just going to have to deal with it." She clapped him on the shoulder, then reached down and plucked her bag from the bed. "We'd better get down there. It would be bad if I was late to the wedding I helped to plan."

Ryder swallowed hard, once again warring with his loyalty to Daniel and his desire for Alex. Luckily, they had somewhere to be. He took her hand. "Come on."

They walked down the grand spiral staircase to the home's central hall, only to run right into Geoffrey Burnett and his wife, Katrina. Geoffrey was a tall and trim man with his head shaved bald. Katrina had a similar willowy build, with glossy silver hair past her shoulders and a quiet elegance about her. They too were dressed for the ceremony, Geoffrey in a tux and Katrina in a pale lavender gown.

"Geoffrey?" Alex asked.

He looked up, surprised. "Yes?" His eyes narrowed. "Are you Chloe's friend? Alexandra? We met at Chloe's graduation."

Alex nodded eagerly while Ryder marveled at Geoffrey's memory. "That's me. You can call me Alex. I want you to meet my boyfriend, Ryder Carson. He's a brilliant architect. He and my brother, Daniel, have their own firm. Perhaps you've heard of it? Gold and Carson?"

Geoffrey thrust his hand in Ryder's direction. "Indeed, I have. It's nice to meet you, Ryder."

"Nice to meet you, too, sir. I'm a huge admirer of yours." There was an awful lot going through Ryder's head right now. He'd waited so long to meet Geoffrey Burnett face-to-face, but funnily enough, the detail he was most fixated on was that Alex had so effortlessly referred to him as her boyfriend. What was between them might not be real, but it sounded so right.

"Please, meet my wife, Katrina." Geoffrey took her hand and pulled her closer as everyone said their hellos.

"Should we walk up to the ceremony together?" Katrina suggested.

"That sounds wonderful," Alex said, turning to Ryder and winking at him. "I know the way."

Outside, they were greeted by a member of the catering staff who was holding a silver tray of glasses of champagne. "Before the ceremony? I love it," Katrina said.

"Yes," Alex replied as Ryder took two glasses, one for him and one for her. "It puts everyone in a much more celebratory mood."

Geoffrey raised his glass to toast. "To love." He eyed Ryder and Alex, then turned his attention to Katrina, looking at her with utter adoration.

"To love," they said in response.

Ryder took a big sip. Who knew Geoffrey Burnett was such a softhearted man? His reputation certainly didn't suggest it.

The four of them started the walk across the sweeping back lawn. They strolled past the rose garden, along a cobbled path through a narrow stretch of woods, and eventually to the clearing where dozens of white chairs were lined up neatly on either side of an aisle runner. At the end of each row was a cascading bundle of magnolia blossoms. "Katrina, did you know that Alex did the floral design for the entire wedding?" Ryder asked as the four sat on the bride's side.

"Is that what you do?" Katrina asked.

"It is. I own my own design shop in Manhattan. It's called Flora," Alex replied.

Katrina slid Geoffrey a look then turned back to Alex. "Do you work on events other than weddings?"

"Of course. We do everything. Birthdays. Corporate parties. Fundraisers."

Katrina reached out and patted Alex's arm. "Remind me to get your number. I might have a job for you."

Alex smiled. "Sounds great."

The officiant took his place before the guests, soon joined by Parker. Alex had explained to Ryder yesterday that Parker and Chloe had wanted a very simple ceremony, without bridesmaids or groomsmen or even flower girls. Just a celebration of the love between them, with friends, family, and a wide-open stretch of blue sky above. When Chloe arrived at the beginning of the aisle, everyone stood, admiring how beautiful, and more importantly, happy, she looked. Ryder didn't know her well, but he knew that if Alex loved Chloe, she was a good person. Step by step, she glided toward Parker, and when she arrived, she hooked her arm in his and the ceremony officially began.

As they sat back down, Ryder noticed that Geoffrey immediately took Katrina's hand, so he did the same with Alex. She smiled thinly at him and he sensed that she was already struggling with what was happening here. He could only imagine how she must be feeling, wondering if her mother had been right about messing up her life by leaving Henry, and possibly thinking about how she would have felt if she had ended up going through with the wedding. He squeezed her hand a little tighter and she squeezed back. In many ways, it felt as though Ryder's heart was compressing right along with it. He couldn't help but feel great compassion for Alex and all she'd been through as he watched her in profile, hanging on every word. She believed in love. He could see it on her face.

When Parker and Chloe began exchanging their vows, Alex's tears came. She was smiling through them, showing the world that she was happy for her friend, but he sensed the melancholy in her. Holding hands was not nearly enough at this point, so he put his arm around her and tugged her close. It reminded him so much of the day he'd run into her before her wedding, when she'd broken down and taken his consoling so readily. The way she seemed to melt into him was just as noticeable now. When it came to a physical connection, they had that part in spades. It was everything else—their circumstances—that seemed to be stacked against them.

Once the happy couple had said "I do," everyone stood again and applauded as Chloe and Parker strode down the aisle with wide smiles on their faces. As the guests all turned to face the aisle, Alex was right in front of Ryder, with her back to him.

He put his hands on her shoulders and leaned down to whisper into her ear. "You okay?" He kept his face close to hear her response.

"I am. Happy. A little sad. Mostly relieved." She craned her neck to look him in the eye and he was so overcome with a need to kiss her. It was this urgent thirst growing inside him, one that could not be denied.

So he did it. It wasn't a long kiss, nor could it be described as white-hot passion. It was a kiss that said they cared about each other. It was a kiss to say that he understood how hard this all was for her. When he pulled back, she froze for a moment with her eyes closed, then the most blissful look crossed her face.

"I'd take another if you're handing those out," she said.

He gave her a kiss all right, this time on her cheek. "Don't push it."

She playfully swatted him on the arm. "I will if I want to."

"Shall we head to the reception?" Katrina asked.

"Yes. I definitely need another drink," Alex said.

The four made their return to the house, where the reception was already showing signs of being in full swing. Champagne was flowing, hors d'oeuvres were being passed, and everyone seemed to be in a jubilant mood, laughing and smiling. Ryder and Alex were able to sit with Geoffrey and Katrina after Alex made a few changes to the seating chart, citing her ability to do whatever she wanted because she'd organized everything.

Over dinner, Alex brought up the subject Ryder had only managed to skirt so far. "So, Geoffrey, I'm sure you don't want to talk too much shop, but I have to tell you about some of the projects that Ryder and my brother have been working on." She delivered the statement with a broad grin and such flat determination that Ryder couldn't imagine Geoffrey saying no.

"Absolutely. Tell me everything," Geoffrey said.

Ryder just sat back as Alex performed every bit of the Gold and Carson pitch he'd prepared, talking up the various builds they'd worked on throughout the city over the last several years. Her knowledge of their work was astounding, but that came as little surprise since she and Daniel were so close. Surely he'd briefed her on as much as she cared to listen to, and apparently, that had been quite a bit. All the while, she told adorable anecdotes about Ryder and Daniel, things that Ryder would not normally share in a business setting. Here, at this wedding, it all came across as perfectly natural and flawless, just like Alex herself.

"You really should hire her to be your firm's spokesperson," Katrina said to Ryder when the spiel was all over.

"And whatever you decide to pay her," Geoffrey added. "Double it."

"Believe me. I know. She's amazing, isn't she?" He looked at her and their gazes locked, sending another jolt of attraction through him. He'd have been lying if he'd said that he wasn't carefully considering forgetting everything he'd promised Daniel.

"You're a very lucky man," Geoffrey said.

"I am." Ryder nodded eagerly, thinking that if he and Alex could be this convincing for this long in front of Geoffrey and Katrina, then perhaps there was something there. They certainly seemed to be in sync. "Alex, since you're so amazing and I'm a lucky guy, would you like to dance?"

A sweet smile crossed her lips. "I would love to."

He took her hand and led her to the dance floor, quickly pulling her into his arms. "Thank you for that. I owe you, big-time. I just couldn't find the right time to mention any of that. I was trying to find an opening, but we're at a wedding. It seemed rude to bring up business or try to brag about what we do."

She shrugged. "It's easy for me to brag about you and my brother."

"It's more than that, though. You're so charming. They're both completely smitten with you. I can tell."

"And how do you feel about me, Ryder?"

I adore you. You're magical. But you're not for me to have. "I appreciate you, Alex. I feel really lucky that we had this weekend together. I feel like we have an even stronger friendship than we did before."

"And what if I don't want to simply be friends?" She delivered the question with a pointed glance.

He drew in a deep breath through his nose, looking away for a moment if only to break the spell she had him under every time she looked at him. He wanted her. But he also wasn't ready to make any promises. "Then I will have to think about that."

"I can't ask for anything more."

He pulled her a little closer and inhaled the sweet smell of her hair. "I promise I won't leave you waiting."

They danced for several more songs, and Ryder greatly appreciated the chance to simply be with Alex and have her in his arms. When they left the dance floor, it gave them a chance to chat with her parents, including her dad, who Ryder hadn't talked to yet. The whole time they were having their conversation, Ryder couldn't escape the feeling that her father was appraising him, trying to sort out whether or not what was between his daughter and him was real. As far as Ryder was concerned, her dad could get in line—he wasn't sure what it was, either.

After two hours, Geoffrey and Katrina said that they'd had enough and were ready for bed. Ryder and Alex offered to walk them back inside to say goodbye.

"It was so great to meet both of you." Ryder shook Geoffrey's hand and then gave Katrina a hug after Alex had done the same.

"Oh, my goodness," Katrina said with a flap of her hand. "It's been our absolute pleasure. You two are a hoot. And really, you're the most darling couple I've seen in a long time." She turned to her husband. "Don't you agree, Geoffrey?"

"I do, darling. I absolutely do. They remind me of us when we were that age." He eyed Ryder and raised his chin as if he was appraising him. Sizing him up. And putting him on edge. "You know, Ryder, I'm thinking we should get together at some point."

"Yes, sir. Can I call you when we get back to the city?"

"Of course. Or I'll call you. I've got your number now. We'll work something out. Good night." With that, Geoffrey and Katrina started down the hall to their room.

Alex slugged him in the arm. "Oh, my God. Ryder. How amazing is that?"

The genuine enthusiasm in her voice was infectious. It only made him want her more. "You're what's amazing. You paved the way for all of that. I couldn't have done it without you. I know I already said this, but you really were so charming. So funny." *So lovely. So sexy. So everything.*

Alex waved it off. "You and my brother are brilliant. It was easy." She turned to look in the direction of the big party still going on outside.

"Do you want to go back to the reception?" He was unsure of the answer he wanted. Part of him was desperate to have her alone. Another part of him knew deep down that it would be a mistake. The problem was that he was on a high right now, one that had been preceded by two days of the utter frustration of being with Alex and not being able to touch her. To say that he needed a break from that hindrance was an understatement.

She turned back to him and shook her head. "Not really. It's pretty obvious to me that Chloe and Parker just want to get to their room. And I think Taylor and Roman are in a similar boat."

"Okay, then." Ryder was dedicated to following Alex's lead here, even though he was torn about what today had been building to—a crescendo that he could only imagine would have him unzipping Alex's dress and breaking a big old promise to her brother.

Six

Alex's heart was pounding as they stepped into their room. It had been a long day and she was exhausted, but mostly she felt like every nerve ending in her body was firing. That was what Ryder did to her. He made her feel that alive. If only he would kiss her for real, like he'd done on their fake date. If only he would let down his guard. "Ryder, I need you to know that I don't say those nice things about you just because you're my brother's friend. I genuinely believe you're brilliant. And you deserve to work with Geoffrey Burnett."

"Still, I can't figure out what I've done to deserve you being so kind to me. I've been pushing you away at every turn."

She shook her head. "Not true. You've been there for me over the last two days, in ways that other people have not. You were there for me after the rehearsal. And last night when we talked. And today, during the ceremony when I got so choked up." She couldn't say that he'd also been there for her the day she called off her wedding. Yet again, it was not a good time to share that secret, and she wasn't sure that time would ever come.

"I can't help it. There's something about you, Alex. Something that makes me want to protect you from everything and everyone who's ever hurt you."

"That's so nice." It was one of the kindest things anyone had ever said to her, but it conjured up those close family feelings, the ones that made him not want to get romantically involved with her.

"It's the truth."

Where was the truth in wanting someone and not being able to have them? That sounded like nothing but wrong. "You know what, Ryder? Please stop talking. Seriously." She inched closer until she was a whisper away from him. Her heart was thumping wildly again, begging for his touch.

"Sorry. Did I say something wrong?"

She looked up into his impossibly warm eyes. They were a swirling kaleidoscope, so difficult to read. Did he see the desire on her face? Was he feeling conflicted again? Hopelessly tied to a promise? "Just kiss me before I explode."

"Alex…"

She shook her head. It probably looked as though she was so sure of herself when she was anything but. "Let me put it this way. If you want to kiss me, please do so. Or I will explode."

A torturous moment passed and then his lips fell on hers, strong and insistent. Slipping his hands around her neck, he cupped her jaw, keeping her face lifted. Close. The kiss was hot and heavenly, his tongue just as sinful as she remembered. The utter relief of having him kiss her like this, when they were all alone, unleashed sheer jubilation inside her. She couldn't believe this was actually happening. She couldn't believe she'd managed to live even a single minute in his presence without this. With every passionate second that ticked by, she was reminded of the pain she'd endured by being near him and not having him. And now? She got to satisfy her hunger.

He gathered her up in his arms and slid his hand to the zipper on the back of her dress, drawing it down. That first brush of his warm hand against her bare skin was enough to send her barreling for her peak. Those nerve endings weren't merely firing now. They were exploding with anticipation. She needed more of him. Now.

She tore off his jacket and threw it to the floor, then unbuttoned his shirt and got rid of that just as fast. Her memory of his gorgeous chest had nothing on the here and now. Remembering every incredible contour and the straight line of his shoulders was nothing compared to being able to touch them.

He pulled the pin from her hair and let it tumble down her back, but then he held it possessively, kissing her neck and the stretch of skin beneath her ear. This was a commanding version of Ryder, taking control, and it was such a turn-on she could hardly believe it. Her shoulders rose in anticipation of what might come next, and as she let them drop, the straps of her dress slumped down to her elbows. He let go of her hair and tugged down the bodice, revealing her breasts. Her nipples went hard from only his attentive gaze. The look in his eyes was more than lust. It was adoration. It was everything she ever wanted in a single look. He took her breasts into his hands gently, kissing each one tenderly before he wound his tongue around one of her nipples. Her skin drew hard and impossibly taught, and she loved that moment when his eyes flashed up at her, telling her without words just how much he loved creating her body's response.

His lips were heavenly on her skin, but she wanted to stretch out next to him, so when he kissed her again, she began walking backward to the bed. With every step, her dress slipped a little lower and she got a little clumsier as she tried to step over the fabric. Not watching where she was going, she bumped into the wall and had to spin on her tiptoes, then step out of her dress. Her bare skin was so attuned to his every touch as his hands roved all over her back and she and Ryder finally landed on the bed with Alex on top.

She immediately went for the button and zipper on his pants, her fingers flying as she pressed her chest into his and took another kiss. She tugged his pants down, and then his boxer briefs, until she had him just as she wanted him. She molded her fingers around his length, feeling the tension in his skin and relishing how ready he was for her. He groaned into her ear, then playfully nipped her lobe, another glimpse of a fiery Ryder she was still so eager to fully know. The next thing she knew, he was wrapping his arms around her waist and flipping her to her back. Then he hovered over her, his white-hot gaze raking across her body. He smiled and dragged a finger across the top edge of her black lace panties, then his lips skimmed over her stomach as he slipped his thumbs beneath the waistband and he cast them aside.

"You're seriously the sexiest woman I have ever met, Alex," he said as he continued to dot her belly with kisses.

For an instant, she thought that if that were really true, she would be impossible to resist. So it couldn't be, because he'd spent so much time doing exactly that—resisting. "I think you already know how I feel about you, Ryder."

"Doesn't mean I don't want to hear you say it," he whispered gruffly.

"I want you. Every inch of you. I want you to bury

yourself in me. I want us to get lost in each other." It felt so good to be flat-out honest, and not hold back.

"I want to get so lost that no one can ever find us."

She grinned to herself, relishing the idea of never having to deal with anyone else's expectations, as he sat back on his knees and trailed his fingers from her knee up along her inner thigh, keeping a light touch, torturing her with every millimeter he traveled. Anticipation took over her entire being as he crept along her skin, knowing where he was going. She reflexively arched her back, wanting him to touch her. Finally.

She gasped when he found her apex and began to tease her delicate folds apart. He then rubbed in small circles with the tips of his fingers, masterfully keeping her under his control by delivering pleasure that was so unbelievable she couldn't quite wrap her head around it. Her eyes fluttered shut as his touch grew firmer. Faster. And more intense. It felt so wonderful to finally experience these things she'd spent the last several months remembering and wishing for, but she wanted to please him as much as he was pleasing her. She pulled his shoulders until he was flat on top of her, weighing her down with his entire body. Then she rolled them to their sides and she took his rock-hard erection in her hand, studying his face as she took strong strokes, loving the way she could make his jaw go slack if she rolled her thumb over his swollen tip.

"You're killing me, Alex," he groaned. "I need you."

She rolled to her back. "If you don't have a condom, I do. In my toiletry kit."

"I have one, too. One second."

She stretched out on the mattress, trying not to think about the reasons why he might have already had a condom with him. He certainly hadn't planned on having sex with her. It didn't matter now. She had him right where she wanted him.

Ryder emerged from the bathroom and approached her with purpose, planting his hands on the bed and crawling along the length of her body. He kissed her stomach again, then reached down between her legs, taking a few quick passes with his fingers before he positioned himself at her entrance. She drew up her knees, wanting him in deep, soaking up that moment when he filled her so perfectly and they began to move in a way that was mutually pleasing. He lowered his head and buried it in her neck, kissing and biting, seeming fitful and unsettled. She dragged her hands up and down his back, feeling every muscled contour, then up over his strong shoulders and finally down to his glorious chest.

Every thrust Ryder took was deep, and the pressure built quickly in Alex's body. In some ways, she felt like she had to hold out, just so she could enjoy every second of what she'd waited so long for. But soon it became too much. He was too much. And the pleasure rolled through her in relentless waves.

She gasped his name and felt her body clutch his as she wrapped her legs around his waist and muscled him closer, just as he froze from his own orgasm, his body tight and tense until he collapsed against her chest, then rolled to his side and kissed her shoulder.

"That was amazing," he said breathlessly. "Worth waiting for."

She turned to him and delivered the hottest, slowest kiss she could manage. "It might have been worth waiting for, but I don't want to wait any longer, Ryder. I still want more."

Despite being in bed with Ryder, Alex checked her phone as soon as she woke up. At first, she was relieved. No new post from Little Black Book. But then that only led her to one conclusion—there was a very good chance that Ruby had been the culprit. But what was the connection? Ruby seemed so meek and sweet. How could someone like that be behind such a vicious and calculating social media account? Not only that, Little Black Book seemed to be everywhere, and yet had never been detected. They were this mysterious figure lurking in the shadows. Did it actually make sense for it to be a woman working for a catering company?

Incredibly, that wasn't the biggest question in Alex's life. Last night with Ryder had been even better than the first time. And if it were up to her, if she could force the stars to align and her brother to get his head out of his ass, she could have more of what she'd had last night. That was the stuff dreams were made of. Specifically, her dreams, although her brain had never managed to whip up a sex dream as hot and fulfilling as last night. The memory of it would be reverberating in her body for a long time. A very long time.

She rolled over to her side and had one good realization. Ryder was still there. He hadn't left her a note or tiptoed away in the middle of the night. Of course, she wasn't sure where exactly he would have gone, but that wasn't the point. The point was that he was still there.

He was also sound asleep. She loved watching him so at peace, with his eyes shut and his perfect mouth a bit slack. She adored him. There was no doubt about that. She'd had her chance for one more taste, but it hadn't satisfied her hunger for him. It only made her want him more, just as badly as she had before she'd kissed him the first time. Even when she was certain that he did not feel the same way.

Was she being self-destructive? Was that what this was? Was there some part of her that just couldn't handle her own happiness so she had a subconscious need to torpedo it? She didn't want to believe that about herself, but if anyone wanted to look at her track record, they'd see the evidence. Between the canceled wedding and her endless pining for a man who'd been clear that he wasn't interested in a relationship, a person could easily wonder if she had a self-defeating streak.

Ryder stirred and rolled toward her, then settled back in, nestling his head in the pillow. She wanted to squeal, he was so adorable and handsome and sexy. But she also knew that she was only going to make things harder on herself later if she continued to stare at him. The next few hours would say a lot about where they stood. Would he panic and run? Or would he want to stick around for more?

"So, uh, how are you this morning?" he mumbled, then opened his eyes but kept them narrowed, as if he might be able to gather visual evidence of how she was feeling. If only he knew that she was simply waiting for the other shoe to drop.

"I'm good. Tired. But relieved the wedding is over."

He hesitated for a moment then nodded slowly. "Right. No more fake boyfriend business."

That was *not* what she was going to say, but since it was front and center in Ryder's thoughts, it made it pretty obvious to Alex that he was already looking for an escape hatch. Yes, they'd slept together, but that was ancient history as far as Ryder was concerned. She could see it on his face.

"Yep. And thank you for filling that role this weekend. I really appreciate it. You did a great job. I think you were probably very convincing." So much so that there had been moments when she had been sure that he wasn't faking it. "Do you feel good about Geoffrey? You guys really hit it off. You must be excited to talk to Daniel about it." She silently cursed herself for bringing up her brother—why did she have to mention the person who wanted so desperately to keep them apart?

He nodded and pinched the bridge of his nose between two fingers. "I do feel good about it. And yes, I can't wait to report back to Daniel. I mean, it's not anywhere close to being a done deal, but I feel as though I made some inroads. I meant what I said last night though, Alex. I owe a lot of that to you. You were wonderful with Katrina and him. You're much more charming than I could ever be."

It felt good to be admired for her personality traits, but this all felt like backpedaling, returning to subjects they'd discussed last night. She wanted to move forward. "I was thinking that we could maybe stay an extra day since it's Labor Day weekend. I'm sure Taylor wouldn't mind."

Ryder ran his hand through his hair and rolled to his back. "Yeah. I don't think that's going to work. The traffic can be horrible on Labor Day and I really feel like I need to get back to the city to catch up with Daniel and with work, especially since I took off most of Friday to come up for this."

Right. Back to work. Back to Daniel. Back to the same old, same old. He was retreating, and as much as Alex disliked it, she was tired of going to great lengths to have him. After last night, if he was going to pass up hot sex because he was worried about traffic, she'd never convince him that she was enough.

Her phone, which was on the bed next to her,

buzzed with a text. When she looked at the message, she saw that it was from her mom. Your father and I are heading out. Can we say goodbye?

"Everything okay?" Ryder asked.

She was really getting tired of that question, especially since the answer was a resounding no. She didn't want to talk to her mom. The afterglow of last night was officially gone. "It's my parents. They're leaving and want me to come downstairs to say goodbye." She typed out her response. Five minutes. Meet me out front?

Sounds good.

"Oh. Your parents. I'd offer to come with you, but I'm not sure I want to see your mom after those things she said about me."

She tossed back the covers, then walked across the room completely naked. If she was going to have to miss out on Ryder, she was going to leave him with a lasting memory, one that was hopefully enough to make him miss her. "No worries. I'll send your best."

"Thank you. I appreciate that. Do you want to leave in an hour?"

Alex grabbed a pair of underwear from her bag and put them on. "Sure thing. Whatever you want." She slipped into a bra, then a knit wrap dress that was both comfortable and sexy. Ryder could admire her breasts in the car all the way home. That would teach him for being so loyal to her brother. She looked back at her suitcase and saw his T-shirt sitting there. She tossed it at him. "Here's your shirt back."

"Thanks," he said, seeming surprised.

"Back in a few." She stepped into the hall and headed downstairs to the foyer, and then outside to the circular driveway. There were a half dozen or so cars out there, guests eagerly getting on the road. Maybe it really was for the best if she and Ryder followed suit. She found her mom and dad at the far side of the parking area, her mom tossing her purse into the front seat while her dad was stuffing suitcases into the trunk of his Mercedes. Even though her parents had more than enough money to buy the latest and greatest of everything, her dad was a big fan of older cars, so this one was from the 1970s, fully loaded and carefully restored to its original beauty. "Hey, you two."

Her dad looked up and smiled, then closed the trunk. "Hey, honey. Just wanted to give my girl a hug before we leave." He wrapped her up in a tight embrace and kissed the top of her head.

At the same time, her mom rounded the car and walked over, spreading her arms wide. "I want one, too."

Alex felt bad for having such negative thoughts about her mom, but she didn't appreciate how meddlesome she could be. "What's next for you and Ryder?" she asked when she stepped back.

Alex nearly laughed. Nearly. "We're going back

to the city. He needs to catch up with Daniel. Work stuff. The usual."

"But nothing romantic?" her dad asked. This was funny because he never weighed in on Alex's love life. Even when Alex had broken things off with Henry, her father said that all he cared about was that Alex was happy. He essentially supported whatever decision Alex chose to make for herself.

Alex shook her head. "I don't think so."

Her mom held her hand to her chest and blew out an exaggerated breath. "That's a huge relief."

"Brigitte. That's not very nice. We love Ryder," her dad said.

Her mother reached for Alex's father's arm. "I know, dear. We do. We absolutely love Ryder. But more as a second son, not a romantic interest for Alex. I just don't think he's right for her, that's all."

Alex folded her arms across her middle. "Well, it's not something you need to worry about, okay?"

"For the record, I wasn't worried. I think Ryder's a great guy," her dad said.

Alex stepped closer to her parents, just to keep things between them. "This conversation is silly in the first place. You both know it's fake and you both know that Daniel would throw a fit."

Her mom pressed her lips together tightly. "I don't know. It didn't look fake on the dance floor. And I saw him kiss you after Chloe and Parker had walked down the aisle. That all looked very real."

It had been. So real. "Like I said, don't worry about it."

"Whatever will make you happy, honey. That's all we really care about." Her dad took her hand and squeezed it one more time.

"Thanks. You two travel safe. Text me when you get home."

Her parents climbed into their car and Alex stood in front of Taylor's family's estate, watching as they drove off, kicking up dust from the crushed-stone driveway. Even her parents were convinced she and Ryder wouldn't work. Well, her dad was essentially neutral on the subject, but Alex didn't need nonanswers. She wanted a yes or a no, even if that meant she was giving in to black-and-white thinking.

Seven

Ryder's phone rang mere minutes after Alex left to say goodbye to her parents. It was Daniel. "Dammit," he mumbled to himself. He impulsively rushed over to his suitcase and grabbed a pair of jeans to put on before he answered. As if Daniel might know from a phone call that Ryder was naked because he'd slept with Alex. "Hey. What's up?" Ryder answered, a bit breathless.

"I'm dying to know what happened with Geoffrey last night. Plus I'm on London time. Sorry if it's too early or you're hung over or something."

Ryder plopped back down on the bed. "Nope. You're good. You'll be happy to know that things with Geoffrey went so much better than I think we could have expected. Alex and I sat with him and his wife during the wedding, then we sat together for the reception, too, all because Alex moved around the seating chart."

"That's such great news. I can't believe you didn't text me right after."

Oh, crap. Delivering an update to Daniel, even a brief one, had not been on Ryder's mind. He'd been far too preoccupied with Alex. "Yeah. Sorry about that. I was wiped out."

"Seems a little weird, but okay."

"Why would you say that?"

"Because you're just as focused on this as I am. And a meeting with Geoffrey Burnett is an absolute coup."

"Well, we don't have an actual meeting set yet. We're going to talk soon. I'm guessing Tuesday. I have his direct number now, though. He said he wants to get together."

"I thought you said it went better than expected. That doesn't sound like better than expected."

"I don't think you understand how much quality time I spent with him. Social time. Hours. I don't think I've ever spent that much purely social time with a client." Ryder was still marveling at everything Alex had done. She deserved some serious props when it came to yesterday. "And by the way, we owe a serious debt of gratitude to your sister. She was a rock star. I hardly had to sell the idea of Gold and Carson to him at all. She sat there and rattled off the details of every major project we've done over the last twenty-four months. It was incredible."

"Why did you let Alex do the talking?"

"Because it just happened that way. And it felt right. Nothing was forced. No heavy sales pitch. I think Geoffrey sincerely appreciated that. And let's be honest, a wedding isn't really the right place to cut a business deal. Chloe and Parker had just had the most important day of their lives. We needed to do some celebrating. It couldn't all be about work."

"Are you feeling okay?"

"Yes. Why would you ask me that?"

"You just don't sound like yourself. I really thought you'd go in for the kill when you were with Geoffrey. That's what you usually do. Get in there and sell it. Sell us."

Ryder wasn't sure how to respond to that. Daniel wasn't entirely off base with his accusation. Normally, Ryder was laser focused on getting what he wanted, which was almost always work related. But this weekend, the spotlight had shifted to Alex. She was not only the real star of the last two days; she'd needed him at times. And that had felt incredibly good. It felt right. He'd never had someone need him in that way *and* accept his help.

"I decided to go with a more natural approach, okay? I think that in the long run, it'll lay a stronger foundation with Geoffrey. I'm going to need you to trust me on this." Ryder put Daniel on speaker, then got back up and returned to his suitcase, hoping for a T-shirt, but quickly realizing the only one he had was the one from MIT. The one sitting on the bed, which Alex had slept in. He trudged back across the room and plucked it from the mattress, then threaded it over his head and put it on. He quickly regretted it. It smelled exactly like her. He might never wash it, if only to hold on to some stronger memories of their weekend. "So just let me make this happen."

"Okay. Fair enough. If it all works out, it will have been worth it for you to go with Alex to the wedding."

Worth it. That was an interesting way to phrase it. It had been more than "worth it" for Ryder. But he had to wonder if Alex would feel the same way. She still ended up in Little Black Book's crosshairs, despite her attempts to mold the narrative about her. Guilt began to close in on him when he thought about what had come after that—last night, and hours of electric connection with Alex, even though he knew that he couldn't give her what she wanted or deserved. He'd not only broken his promise to his best friend. He'd broken his promise to himself about not hurting Alex. "I think it will all work out." Or so he hoped.

"Speaking of Alex, is she around?"

"She's downstairs saying goodbye to your parents."

"Oh, boy. My mom totally has it in her head that you two are an actual couple. And she keeps saying how she loves you, but you two would never be right for each other. Of course, I told her that it wouldn't happen. You and I are too tight. Our friendship is too strong for that."

Ryder swallowed hard. "Maybe your mom thinks that because Alex and I are good at putting on a show. And maybe she thinks that because no one will ever be good enough for her daughter."

"My mom thought Henry was good enough. More than good. She thought he was perfect for her."

Fire was starting to burn in the pit of Ryder's stomach. "Isn't it more important that Alex decide who's perfect for her?"

"I guess. Try convincing my mom of that, though. It won't be easy." He cleared his throat. "Anyway, I don't want you to think I don't appreciate you doing this. Taking one for the team and all of that."

Take one for the team? Ryder felt even lower now. How had he allowed himself to get into such a mess? Things would be so much simpler if he'd stayed on the straight and narrow last night and not slept with Alex. Although he wasn't sure how he was supposed to resist her. She had this power over him, and although he never liked to let a professional adversary get the upper hand, he had no problem giving everything to her. Maybe he was losing his touch. "I'll see you back at the office?"

"Yes, you will. But please call me if you talk to Geoffrey before then. Just get a meeting on the schedule, okay?"

"I will." Ryder said goodbye and hung up the

phone. He had an urge to flop back on the bed. Maybe punch a pillow. He couldn't remember a time he'd been more frustrated. He was genuinely happy about the progress he'd made with Geoffrey. But that clearly wasn't enough.

His phone rang again and he grabbed it but didn't look, assuming it would be Daniel. "Hey. What's up?"

"I had a day off, so I thought I'd call you." It was Ryder's father.

"Dad. Hi." He sat up straighter. All these years later and the man still commanded his attention in a way that was so visceral. Ryder wanted nothing less than to please him. To prove himself. "How are you?"

"I'd be a lot better if I didn't have to see my son kissing some rich girl on the internet. Damn Nancy next-door sent it to me. You're humiliating yourself. What in the hell are you doing?"

Ryder's stick-straight posture crumpled. "That's Alex, Dad. Daniel's sister. She's not some rich girl. She's a very nice person. You like Daniel. I'm sure you would like her, too."

"Is it serious? Are you thinking you're going to marry her? Because she left that other guy at the altar. So I don't really see how you're supposed to measure up. Might be time to cut bait."

Alex opened the door and walked into the room. Ryder quickly stood and put his phone on mute. "It's my dad. I'll just be a sec."

"Do you need me to leave?"

He didn't want Alex to overhear the conversation, but he also wasn't about to kick her out of their room. He'd just have to tiptoe around certain words with his dad. "No. No. It's fine."

"I'll go brush my teeth."

That would buy him a minute or so. "Great." He unmuted his phone as soon as he heard Alex running the water in the bathroom. "Dad. Sorry. I'm away at a wedding, actually. I just had to speak to someone."

"Oh, I get it. I'm second in the pecking order."

"That's not true. At all."

"Well, I also wanted to let you know that I won't need that September check, so don't even bother sending it."

"Why?"

"Because it's just me and the house is paid for and I haven't spent the last money you sent."

"So? Do something nice for yourself. Take a trip. Put money down on a new car. You deserve it. You've worked hard your whole life."

"Those things aren't important to me, son. You know that."

Ryder blew out a resigned breath. "I know."

"I don't need to get on a plane and stay in a fancy hotel to enjoy myself."

"So buy a tent and go fishing. Or better yet, let me buy you an RV."

"No, thank you. Don't think I don't appreciate you being generous. I do. But that's not me. I'd just get bored. And they need me at work."

Ryder had to admire the man, as difficult as he could be. He knew what he wanted and he had a work ethic that was built into his very fiber. Ryder got that from him—that will to put everything into your livelihood and leave no doubt that you'd tried your absolute hardest. "I'm going to take September's check and put it in that investment account I set up for you. It's there whenever you need it. Your choice."

"I won't need it. But thank you. And keep a watch on yourself. I don't want you caught up with that woman who dumped her fiancé. You deserve better than that."

If only he could tell his dad the reality of the situation—that he'd be lucky to have Alex. She was the most incredible woman he'd ever met. She simply wasn't his to have. "I'll keep that in mind."

"I'd better go. Lots to get done around the house today."

Ryder knew that was a lie. His dad was probably going to watch football all day. "Sure. Of course."

"Goodbye, Ryder. Love you."

"I love you, too, Dad." Ryder hung up the phone and looked up. Alex was standing in the bathroom doorway.

"Everything okay?"

Where to begin? Everything wasn't okay. It was all messy and complicated, which Ryder detested. A little bad. A little good. And there in the middle was Alex—perfect in every way, except that her amazing qualities left her out of reach. There was some truth to what his dad was getting at. Alex was from a different world, and even though Ryder lived there now, it wasn't his core. Work was his foundation, and Daniel was an essential part of that. "Yep. Everything's great."

"Okay. I'll get packed up."

"Me too."

They were out the door a half hour later, and said many goodbyes in the driveway. There were Chloe and Parker, who weren't going on their honeymoon until January, when they could take a serious chunk of time off and trade the city in winter for a beach on a tropical island. And Taylor and Roman, who were now about to embark on the real renovation of the estate, all in preparation for Taylor to open it as a boutique hotel. There was talk of Little Black Book, too, of course. Parker already had a private investigator looking for Ruby. He made a point of telling Ryder that he'd loop him in on whatever he discovered. That was one bright spot—Parker and Roman had been nothing less than welcoming to Ryder. He already considered them friends, which was nice. In this world, money and professional accolades didn't get you friendship. They got you connections. Ryder had plenty of connections, but aside from Daniel, his friend circle was relatively small.

The first half hour of the ride back to the city was virtually silent, aside from the playlist Alex had going in the background as she tapped away on her phone or sometimes simply looked out the window.

That left Ryder to his thoughts, which wasn't a pleasant experience. All he could think about was what Daniel and his dad had put in front of him that morning, even if neither of them knew it. They were two strong reminders that Ryder needed to get back on track with the things that worked best for him—his career and his friendship with Daniel. He wanted Alex desperately, but she wasn't meant for him. But how was he supposed to coax his relationship with Alex back to where it had been when they'd climbed into his car two days ago? And how could he do that without hurting her feelings?

"How was your mom when you said goodbye? Still being a pain in your butt?" he asked.

"Oh, of course. She doesn't know how to do anything else. Doesn't mean I don't love her. I do."

"I spoke to Daniel this morning. Right after you went downstairs. Got him caught up on everything with Geoffrey. I told him we owed a lot of it to you."

"I guess that means our fake wedding date ultimately worked."

"It did. It definitely did." Ryder was scrambling to find the best way to say what he needed to say. His mind was a torrent of words, all of them hard to utter. The last thing he wanted to do was hurt her in any way. She'd already been through so much. "Alex—"

Her phone rang. "Oh. Wow."

"Who is it?"

"Katrina."

Hmm. This was an interesting development. "Oh. Cool. Answer it."

"I'll put her on speaker." Alex pressed the button and held out her phone so Ryder could hear and speak, too. "Katrina? What's going on?"

"Geoffrey and I just got back to the city and we started talking about you two."

Alex glanced at Ryder, her eyes wide with surprise. "Oh. How nice. Ryder and I really had a great time with you two at the wedding. He's right here in the car with me."

"Hi, Katrina," Ryder said.

"Oh, perfect," Katrina replied. "I'm glad I get to speak to you both. Geoffrey mentioned how he'd told you, Ryder, that he wanted to get together."

"Yes." *Oh, thank God.* He could get Daniel off his back. Or…was that what this was? If Geoffrey wanted to set up a work meeting, why wasn't he calling?

"We were thinking this week if that works for your schedules? We'd love to have you two over to our place. A nice intimate dinner. Just the four of us?"

So *that* was the invitation Geoffrey had extended. "Get together" meant something social with Alex and him, not a business meeting with Daniel. Ryder clearly hadn't made the progress that he thought he had. That was going to be a nightmare to break to Daniel, but he had no choice going forward. He had to make something out of this. "Sounds great to me."

He looked over at Alex. "What's your schedule like, uh, honey?"

She twisted her lips into a bundle, telling him with a single expression that his use of a pet name had not come out smoothly. "It's a short week, so maybe Friday night? Would that work?" Alex asked.

"That's good for me," Ryder added. It wasn't like he had some extensive social schedule. Most Fridays were for working late.

"That's great. Geoffrey works a half day on Fridays. I'm trying to slowly nudge him into retirement. Shall we say seven o'clock? Our place? We're in the One 57 building. I'll text you the address."

Alex and Ryder made eye contact one more time. She was asking if this was okay. He was, too. He needed to know if she was good with all of this. Ostensibly, there wasn't anything in this for her. "Sounds great," Alex answered. "We'll be there."

Ryder exhaled. On one hand, he could postpone his serious conversation with Alex. On the other hand, this would mean more time together where they pretended to be a couple. It was an easy role for him to play, but that was the problem. If this was all getting jumbled in his head and heart, surely Alex felt the same way. And that meant that someone would ultimately get hurt. "Can we bring anything?"

"Just yourselves. Geoffrey will be so excited. See you Friday."

"Bye, Katrina," they said in unison.

"Bye-bye."

Alex hung up the phone. "Wow. They're obsessed with us."

Ryder laughed, thankful that she'd lightened the mood. "We *are* a very fun couple."

She smiled so adorably that he wanted to kiss her. Pull off the road and lay one on her. "The most fun. I mean, who wouldn't want to hang out with us?"

"Only people with very poor taste in friends."

A breathy laugh escaped Alex's lips. "How's Daniel going to take this? Is he going to be mad that you're basically Geoffrey Burnett's new best friend?"

Ryder shook his head as he kept his eyes trained on the road, still absorbing this peculiar twist in the state of affairs. "I really don't know. I'm guessing he's not going to be happy that our fake relationship is going beyond this weekend. I think he was okay with it because it was a finite amount of time."

Alex shrugged. "I doubt he'll be mad. He'll be annoyed, but not mad."

"How so?"

"He won't care about you and me as long as it's leading to a greater chance of you guys landing Geoffrey as a client. That's all he's concerned with."

"That's not necessarily true. He called me the morning we left for the wedding, freaking out about that photo in the tabloids of us kissing. He said it looked entirely too real. It really made him uncomfortable."

"Wow."

Ryder nodded. "Oh, yes. He made it crystal clear how much he did not like it."

Alex sighed and sank back in her seat. "That's his problem, Ryder. We've been through this one hundred times. If he doesn't like it, there's nothing you or I can do about that."

"Except, perhaps, *not* kiss each other."

"And exactly how good have we been at that?"

"Not very good." Ryder's mind was once again a whirlwind of competing thoughts. Mere seconds ago, he'd wanted to kiss her. And if he was being honest right now, he still did. Why did he so badly want what wasn't a good idea? "You know, it's easy for you to tell your brother to butt out. It's not such a simple thing for me."

"Why not?"

"Because you're his sister. Blood really is thicker than water. He has to listen to you eventually. And he loves you to death. I don't have that advantage."

"My brother loves you. He does."

"I know. And I love him, too. But we also run a multimillion-dollar company together. Dozens of people rely on us for a paycheck. For their careers. And their families. It's not a small matter if he and I aren't on the same page. If we aren't getting along."

"I guess I never really looked at it like that. I suppose it is more than simply telling Daniel to get over it, huh?"

"Unfortunately, yes. And everything blows up if he decides he hates me because I broke my promise to him." It was the truth. Gold and Carson would be toast. Gone. And then where would Ryder be? In an incredibly uncertain and lonely place.

"I wish you'd never made the promise to begin with."

"Maybe I shouldn't have. But when your best friend asks you to do something, you do it. Even if you know it might hurt you. You said yes to Chloe when she asked you to organize her wedding. Even though you knew that it was going to be triggering for you."

"Yes, but that was a one-time thing. It's not like she asked me to organize her wedding for all of eternity. What my brother asked of you is a lot. I mean, if you actually like me."

Ryder squeezed the steering wheel a little tighter. "Of course I like you."

"But? I sense a but."

He had a whole lot of reservations. He wasn't about to list them for her now. "Last night was amazing. The whole weekend was great. I can't remember a time when I had more fun."

"Really?"

He hated how much hope was in her voice there. No matter how much he liked her or cared about her, he didn't see this going anywhere. The obstacle with Daniel really was too great a hill to climb. But still, he couldn't lie to her about how he felt. "Really."

"So where does that leave us?"

Us. It was an interesting word choice. "Well, we

have somewhere to go together on Friday night. As for me, I'm going to have to figure out if I can even look your brother in the eye this week, knowing that I wasn't honest with him. I made a promise. And then I broke it."

"I'm sorry you have to deal with that. I feel like a lot of it is my fault."

"No. I'm sorry. It's my burden to bear."

Alex got quiet again. She picked at her nails and glanced out the window. "I like you a lot, Ryder. I'd be lying if I said that this weekend didn't mean a lot to me, especially last night."

Ryder wasn't sure what to say in response. He had similar feelings, but there was something deep inside of him that was saying he needed to keep this from going any further. Having heart-to-heart conversations with Alex and admitting to feelings was a one-way road to a far more serious place. And ultimately, the deeper they got with each other, the more difficult it was going to be when it didn't work out. He didn't want this all to end in a place where he and Alex weren't still friends. That would be devastating. It might kill him. "Look. I don't think you or I should make promises to each other right now. Let's enjoy ourselves on Friday night. I don't want to think beyond that."

"Because it's easier?"

"Honestly? Yes."

She waited for several moments before she answered. "Okay. But then that means you're in the driver's seat. Literally and figuratively. If you want more of me, you're going to have to say it. Out loud. With clear words and an open heart. Anything beyond that, you're going to have to figure out your situation with my brother at some point. I can't do it for you two."

Ryder was more than a little surprised to hear this assertive version of Alex. He liked it. A lot. Despite the fact that she was completely putting him on the spot, it was a total turn-on. "I can live with that."

"Good. Kiss me or not on Friday, Ryder. It's all up to you."

Eight

It's all up to you. Those had not only been Alex's words to Ryder when they were driving back from the wedding, they were the basic theme of Ryder's four days back in the office with Daniel. He'd gone absolutely ballistic when Ryder first told him that Geoffrey didn't want to meet, but instead wanted more social time, which would not include Daniel. To make matters worse, it made Alex an essential piece of the puzzle, and once again put Ryder's fake relationship with her at center stage. Daniel's response to it all was, "Figure it out or this whole ridiculous thing will have been for nothing."

Daniel seemed to have become blind to what his sister had originally wanted from the fake date to the wedding—to rehab, or at the very least, protect her online reputation. And no, that hadn't worked out quite like she thought it would, but it wasn't for nothing that they'd tried to join efforts to protect her. Ryder had attempted to point this out, but it only aroused suspicion. "You don't seem to be concerned enough about the business ramifications of what hasn't happened," Daniel snapped.

Ryder quickly assured him that he was very concerned and that he'd do his best to corner Geoffrey when the opportunity arose. Now that it was Friday, the heat was really on.

"I still don't understand why Geoffrey didn't ask for a business meeting." Daniel had stepped into Ryder's office, not asking whether or not he might be interrupting something. That was how badly this subject was bothering Daniel. He was like a dog with a bone. He could not leave it alone, and it was making him quite grumpy. Normally, he was quite considerate and understanding.

Ryder was packing up his laptop and glanced at the clock. He needed to be at Alex's in an hour, meaning he didn't have time to rehash the topic at any great length. Nor did he want to rehash it for the fiftieth time. "Daniel. We've been through this. Alex and I were together at the wedding, we met Geoffrey and Katrina at the wedding and there was no real way to make it anything other than a package deal. I still believe he's interested in working with us. I really do. Tonight, I will do my best to pin him down for an actual meeting."

"Okay. Well, I've thought about it and there's another problem we have."

Another? How was that possible? "What is it?"

"At some point, Geoffrey and his wife are going to find out that you aren't a real couple. What are we supposed to do then?"

That thought had not occurred to Ryder, and he didn't have the mental bandwidth to think it through now. "I'm not sure, exactly. I guess she and I will just have to quietly break up at some point. Possibly months from now." He cleared his throat, waiting for a response.

"Months? Are you serious?"

"I don't know, Daniel. You're speaking in hypotheticals, and all I can deal with is what's right in front of me. I need to get home so I can change and pick up Alex for our dinner date."

"You mean your fake dinner date."

"I'm pretty sure the Burnetts won't be serving fake food."

"Don't joke around about this. It's serious."

It was a curious thing, but ever since Alex had accused Ryder of black-and-white thinking, he was starting to see it more and more. Sometimes it was in his own view of the world. Other times, like now, the perspective belonged to someone else—namely, Daniel. "I need to go or I'm going to be late. I don't want to leave Geoffrey and his wife waiting."

"Or my sister, for that matter."

"Or your sister." Ryder stepped past Daniel, out into the hall.

Daniel followed him to Reception. "All right. Well, let me know what happens. Send me a text or something. I've kept my schedule as clear as possible for next week. It would be great if we could get him in here right away. I know for a fact that there are other firms chasing him."

"I will do my best. I promise."

Daniel clapped him on the shoulder. "I know you will. I'm sorry if I'm being a pain. I know you're working your tail off. Hopefully it will all pan out."

Ryder was nowhere close to being sure of any of that, but he wasn't about to voice his reservations. He headed downstairs to the parking deck and hopped in his car, then drove from the Gold and Carson offices near the Flatiron building to his apartment on Bleecker Street in the NoHo neighborhood. He'd bought his penthouse six years ago, when it was clear that Gold and Carson was going to continue to grow by leaps and bounds. The neighborhood had become exponentially more hip and popular since he moved in, meaning his property value had gone through the roof. It was a wise investment that afforded him another layer of security.

After a quick shower, he dressed in a charcoal-gray suit and white shirt—nothing too casual or outlandish for their evening with the Burnetts. As he ran a comb through his hair one last time, he did wonder what Alex was going to wear that night… and exactly how hard she would be to resist because of it. Although one could argue that it might be best for Ryder to drive them himself so he could have the distraction of keeping his eyes trained on the road, he ultimately decided to book a limo for the occasion. Alex deserved the best. And he couldn't deny that he wanted as much time alone with her as he could get. They hadn't seen each other in five days and he could admit to himself that he missed her.

It was a relatively quick ride across town to Alex's building, despite a bit of Friday early evening traffic. This time, he skipped the parking garage and had his driver pull up in front of her building. He sent her a text. I'm out front. Anytime you're ready.

Not in the parking garage?

Nope. We have a limo tonight.

You clever boy. Down in a minute.

He found himself grinning like a fool at his phone. It was a text from Alex. This was not a big revelation in his life. But it did make him happy. He quickly climbed out of the car and strode inside to wait for her outside the elevator. When the doors slid open, she looked up and her gaze locked in on his like it was the only place there was to look. It was like a bolt of lightning square in the chest with enough force to blow him across her building's lobby and into a wall. *Wow*. He knew he'd missed her this week, but now he was beginning to understand the depths of that feeling. He drank in the vision of Alex in an elegant but criminally sexy body-hugging sleeveless white dress, with a high neck that on the surface seemed quite demure but left Ryder thinking about exactly what that stretch of fabric was hiding. There was a small cluster of shiny silver beads at her nipped-in waist, and the skirt skimmed her hips so perfectly that he could hardly tell where the dress ended and she began. Tonight was going to be an exercise in restraint, at least for the first part. She'd put the ball in his court. It might be time to whack it back.

"Ryder. You didn't have to come inside," she said as the elevator doors closed behind her.

"What kind of fake boyfriend would I be if I did that?"

She leaned in and kissed him on the cheek. "Thanks. It's nice to know you're making an effort." She slipped her arm into the crook of his. "Let's go."

They rode north up to 57th Street and Billionaire's Row, where the Burnetts had an apartment in the same building Taylor's boyfriend, Roman Scott, did. It was one of the most exclusive addresses in the city, and like many of the newer supertall buildings in this part of the city, it had unprecedented views of Central Park. Ryder found it egregious on both an architectural level and from a personal standpoint—

the buildings were cold and lifeless towers of steel and glass that cast long dark shadows on the urban oasis of the park below. Living in a building like this was a game Ryder could afford to play, but chose not to. He couldn't see himself rubbing shoulders with what would be his fellow residents. But knowing that Roman lived here, as well as the Burnetts, and thinking about how much he liked all three of them, certainly made him rethink his attitudes. His dad loved to look down on the wealthy, but he didn't know anyone in this world other than Ryder. Not everyone with money was a selfish snob.

When they arrived at the Burnetts' door, both Katrina and Geoffrey answered. Their faces positively lit up when they saw Ryder and Alex, and they were quick to welcome them inside. Katrina instantly pulled Alex into a hug, while Ryder shook hands with Geoffrey.

"Please. Come on in," Geoffrey said.

"Wow. What a beautiful place," Alex said, looking to the windows opposite the foyer, with that unmatched Central Park view. It was like being up in the clouds.

"I would love to give you a tour," Katrina said. "We've put a lot of time into decorating and I love to show it off."

Alex looked at Ryder then returned her attention to their host. "Absolutely. Lead the way."

Katrina started down the hallway to their right, with Alex and Ryder following close behind and

Geoffrey bringing up the rear. She pointed out several bedrooms and a powder room, then an office and the owner's suite. "On the way into the kitchen and living area, we have our gallery hall."

"She's very proud of the gallery," Geoffrey said.

Katrina came to a stop and planted a hand on her hip. "There's a reason for that. It's a chronicle of our lives together. Since we mutually decided to never have kids, this is as close as we get to showing off our family."

"That's true. And I love it. I'm sorry if it sounded like I was making fun of it," Geoffrey said.

Katrina stepped aside, allowing Alex and Ryder to proceed down the corridor. Dozens and dozens of photographs lined the walls on either side, each carefully matted and framed. To Ryder's great surprise, he recognized many of the people in the pictures—they were former presidents, famous actors, well-known figures from history, and even rock stars. Katrina and Geoffrey were beyond well-connected. Ryder couldn't help but think about the photographs that had been in the hall back at home in Boston when he was growing up. There were only two—one of Ryder with his grandmother on his eighth birthday, and another of Ryder's mother, the woman he'd never known because she'd died soon after he was born. He often felt as though he had very few close ties in the world, which was why his relationship with Daniel and Daniel's family, including Alex, was so important.

A buzzer in the other room went off. "Oh. That's dinner. Geoffrey, can you give me a hand with the steaks?" Katrina asked.

"We'll be back in a few," Geoffrey said to Ryder. "Please feel free to poke around."

As soon as they were gone, Ryder had to comment. "Pretty amazing that they know all of these people, huh?"

"It is. But I try not to be too starstruck. They're just people."

He looked over at her as she examined the photographs. He was almost starstruck by her, or at the very least in awe. Being with her made the whole world look different. He'd noticed a change in himself this week at work, where he found himself daydreaming about her, or times when he felt less uptight about work. He could see himself slowing down at some point—not a lot, but a little, and that was no small development for him. He even found himself taking work a little less seriously. Alex did this to him—she forced him to question things. Including himself and his priorities. "I suppose. Or maybe it's just that you grew up in a world where you could see famous people that way."

She placed her hand on his back. "And you didn't."

He appreciated that she didn't gloss over or minimize what his life had been like before he'd met her and her family. She also never judged him for having come from humbler beginnings. "Right. I'm not sad about it. It's just a very, very different perspective."

Alex brushed a piece of lint from his jacket. "For the record, I love your perspective. I love seeing how your brain works."

Funny, but he'd just been thinking the exact same thing about her. And although love was an awfully strong word, it resonated in his body, a low and warm hum that was impossible to ignore. "Oh, yeah?"

"Believe it or not, I don't just like you for your hot bod, Ryder. I also like you for your smarts." She tapped the side of his head with her finger.

He grinned, searching for the perfect response while he was temporarily hypnotized by her lips. "Is this part of you putting the ball in my court?"

"I wouldn't say putting. More like launching. Like I'm one of those machines that spits out tennis balls."

Message received, loud and clear. "Okay. Then let me return the serve." He wrapped an arm around her waist and tugged her close, delivering a kiss that he hoped would leave her with the same bodily hum she'd given him. It was hot and wet, making him lose all sense of time and place, all while making him feel as though this was exactly where he was meant to be.

"Geoffrey, look at these two lovebirds," Katrina's voice came from behind him.

Ryder broke the kiss and whipped around, but he still kept Alex in his arms as heat flooded his face. "Sorry."

"Don't be. Geoffrey and I used to be the same way." Katrina turned back. "Come on. Let me show off the kitchen."

* * *

Dinner with Geoffrey and Katrina was suitably elegant and indulgent—filet mignon, French green beans with cracked black pepper and garlic, along with the most decadent potatoes au gratin Alex had ever allowed to cross her lips. Geoffrey had a sizable wine collection in the apartment, complete with a few vintages Ryder was very impressed by, which Geoffrey gladly opened. Not that Alex was paying that much attention. She greatly enjoyed Geoffrey and Katrina's company, but her focus was on the wait she had to endure until she could learn what came after that kiss Ryder had given her in the hall. Holy smokes, it was hot. The kiss had *subtext*. It was saying something, and she had an inkling what it might be, but she was also hesitant to do her own translation. She really wanted Ryder to lay it all out there for her, so she could finally learn what his body had to say to hers.

"So, Alex," Katrina said as she delivered dessert, a crème brûlée with fresh berries. "I loved your floral designs for Chloe's wedding. I'd really like to talk to you about working on a fundraiser I'm coordinating. Would you be interested?"

Alex took a bite of her dessert first, a silky vanilla and burnt sugar treat. She wanted to discuss flowers, but she also had personal priorities that often revolved around sweets. "Absolutely I'm interested. Come into my shop anytime so we can talk about it."

"What about next week? Would Friday at 1:00 work?"

Alex was surprised Katrina wanted to move so quickly, but she was eager to work on the project. "Absolutely. I'll clear my schedule."

"Wonderful. That's all set then." Katrina turned to Geoffrey and gave him a side-eye.

Geoffrey cleared his throat. "This is the part where my wife wants me to discuss business with you, Ryder, but you know, I'd really prefer to talk about it when I'm in the office. Maybe next week?"

"Oh. Yeah. Of course. Absolutely no problem." Ryder waved it off as if it was nothing, when Alex knew that it wasn't the case at all.

"It's not as simple as flowers," Geoffrey said in return.

"Hey," Alex protested, wanting to lighten the mood. She hated that Geoffrey had put off Ryder again, but she did have faith that it would eventually work out. "Flowers aren't that simple."

"Alex is right," Ryder said, looking at her and smiling. "Flowers are actually quite complicated. And as for your work and mine, I know we could do an excellent job for you. But I also believe that if it's meant to be, it's meant to be."

Alex froze for a moment, wondering if she'd just heard that come out of Ryder's mouth. Mr. Black-and-White was being so...philosophical. He seemed so willing to let things play out. She admired this new side of him. As to whether it might stick, she wasn't sure.

"Point taken," Geoffrey said. "I appreciate that."

Katrina quickly changed the subject, bringing up an art exhibit she was excited to see, which eventually led to them talking about their apartment again, which then brought them around to how much the city had changed in the last decade. It gave Ryder the perfect opening to talk about his work, but he didn't take the bait. Instead, he licked the back of his spoon after his final bite of dessert, and delivered a penetrating look in Alex's direction. She could feel the heat radiating from him and she wanted to get swallowed up by it. She also wanted to understand how he had so much self-control. She'd gobbled up her creme brûlée a good fifteen minutes earlier.

"So, Ryder," Geoffrey said. "When are you going to put a ring on Alex's finger?"

Alex had not expected this at all, but she felt like she had to intervene. "We haven't been together that long, Geoffrey. Plus, if you read the tabloids, I'm to be avoided when it comes to matrimony."

"Don't say that about yourself, Alex," Katrina interjected. "Ryder would be lucky to have you for his wife. And you two really make the most adorable couple."

Ryder eyed Alex, although she couldn't sort out what his expression was saying. "It's true. I would be lucky."

Eager to get out of there, Alex conjured a fake

yawn, placing her hand over her mouth, but making quite a lot of noise. "I am so sorry, everyone. I'm just wiped out. It was a very long day at Flora. We should probably excuse ourselves." She turned to Ryder. "Ready?"

"Yes." The dining chair scraped against the hardwood floor when he popped up from his seated position. She loved seeing that response. She couldn't wait to get back into that limo.

The four all said goodbye at the door, then Ryder and Alex walked swiftly to the elevator. They were all alone when they got there, both turning to face the doors when they slid closed. Her heart was beating like a wild animal. Her breaths were shallow, and her blood running hot. She wanted to flatten him against the wall and kiss him silly, but she'd promised herself she would not do that. She wanted him to take the lead.

And then he did. He made one stealth step behind her, placed one hand on her shoulder while the other swept her hair back. He kissed her cheek quite close to her ear, then down to her jaw, and finally her neck. His mouth was so hot and heavenly against her skin, and she found herself wishing for the longest elevator ride in history. Perhaps there was some button she could push? One that would let them ride up and down all night while he continued to kiss her neck?

As for buttons, he shifted his other hand to her waist, then slid it lower, grazing her center through her dress and panties. A buzz ran through her; she moaned softly from his teasing touch and then the elevator dinged. Ryder stood straight and cleared his throat. Alex blinked frantically while she struggled for her composure. She was more than a little bit dizzy. Luckily, he took her hand as soon as the doors were all the way open, and strode with her through the building's lobby and outside to the waiting car.

As they climbed into the back seat, Alex again wondered what was waiting for her. She'd never had sex in a limousine, and she wasn't sure Ryder was the type, but if he wanted to try it, she was game. They got situated and he took her hand again. "Alex, where are we going? Your place?"

That would not be her first choice. He'd hurt her feelings pretty badly the time they'd had sex there. "I'd like to go to your apartment. I've never been there."

"Perfect." He reached over for the button that lowered the privacy partition between them and the driver. "We're going to my apartment," he said.

"Yes, sir," the driver replied.

Ryder raised the partition again and turned to Alex, digging his fingers into her hair and raising her mouth to his. "The hall was only the start, Alex. I have to have you." He kissed her softly, but deeply, teasing her with his tongue.

She loved having him take the lead, but she wanted to keep a straight head about this. She'd failed to speak her mind when it came to Henry. She wasn't going to make that mistake again. "I want you, too. But I need to know now that we can move forward from this. I won't be a secret forever, Ryder. If this is going to happen again, I want it to happen a lot. And that means things are going to get messy. Are you ready to do that?" She peered up into his eyes, scanning his face, searching for clues as to what he was really thinking.

"You know how I hate blurring the lines. But if I'm going to do it with anyone, I would want it to be with you."

Nine

Ryder wasted no time when they got to his apartment. He locked the door, cast aside his jacket and set her evening bag on the table in the foyer. "I vote we start the tour in my bedroom. If that's okay with you."

Alex laughed quietly. "That's exactly what I would have suggested, but you're in charge, so it's even better."

He smiled to himself. "Good. It's straight ahead. Down the hall. The very end."

She took a step then looked back at him over her shoulder, her eyes glinting with mischief. "This way?"

"You've got it. Keep going."

She took a few more steps before he began to walk behind her. He wanted to watch her spectacular ass in motion, her hips swaying from side to side in that white dress. Finally they reached his bedroom and she walked right in with purpose, then stopped in the center of the room again peering back at him with a look that told him that there was no more need for self-control. That was all out the window. "I like what I've seen so far."

"I like what I've seen of you in that dress." His hands burned with the need to touch her. "But I want to see more."

She turned to him, her luminous skin brought to light by the soft shadows of moonlight through the windows. "I practically handed you that line, didn't I?"

"Oh, I would have said it even without the perfect introduction. The words were sitting on my lips all damn night."

"But you thought it might be strange to say at the dining room table?" She reached up and rested her forearms on his shoulders.

His hands immediately went to her waist, then he caressed her full hips. "I know the Burnetts love us, but I didn't want to push it too far."

She laughed quietly and even in the low light of the room, he could have sworn he saw her eyes sparkle. It sucked the breath right out of him. "You surprised me tonight, Ryder. I can't believe you didn't push Geoffrey about your meeting. The Ryder of, oh, one week ago, would have done that. And he wouldn't have let go until he had what he wanted."

"Ah. That's where you've misread me. I'm still just as determined to get what I want. But after four days of not seeing you? I don't give a damn about a meeting. What I want is you."

She shook her head from side to side, slow, like the drip of honey. "You are amazing. You never fail to say the perfect thing."

He wasn't swayed by flattery, but kind words from Alex were worth so much more than from anyone else. "You're the one who's amazing. Resilient. Tough."

"I'm not entirely tough." She reached down to the hem of her skirt and lifted it as high as her hip. "Parts of me are soft."

He did not need any more invitation than that, but he also relished the thought of surprising her again, so he dropped to his knees before her and slowly pushed the fabric of her dress up to her waist. Every new inch of her skin revealed felt like a gift, even when he'd seen her beautiful body before. It all felt so new and special. He tugged down her silky panties, then gently touched her center with his finger. It was a soft brush, much like the one in the elevator. He wanted to nudge her toward pleasure and let her enjoy every incredible step along the way. She gasped when he did it a second time, then he leaned forward and kissed her there, tasting her sweetness as he swirled his tongue and she dug her fingers into his hair. Everything about Alex was a total turn-on, but pleasing her was next-level. It made his dick hard and hot. He needed her like nothing else.

He stood and stepped behind her, drawing down the zipper of her dress, again loving the feeling of revealing a treasure. He pressed his body against hers, his fierce erection nestled between their bodies. He was at war with himself, wanting his clothes off, wanting her clothes gone, but still wanting to savor every delicious moment of buildup. He nudged her dress from her shoulders and she pulled it down in the front, far enough that it began to slide past her hips and eventually fell to the floor. He wrapped his arms around her bare waist, pulling her back against him, his hands cupping her full and luscious breasts, the silky fabric smooth against his palms. He skimmed his lips over the soft skin of her neck and she dropped her head to the side just as she had in the elevator, moaning in pleasure, urging him on. He brought his hands back to unhook her bra while still kissing her neck as she pulled the garment from her body.

He turned her around, cupping her naked breasts with his hands, her skin impossibly warm beneath his touch. He lowered his head to lick and suck her hard nipples, the skin tightening with every pass of his tongue. Her frantic fingers went to work on his shirt while he kept his attention focused on her breasts. He could touch them for hours, but he had to let go long enough to unbutton his cuffs and peel off his shirt. He reached for Alex, but she surprised him with the exact same move he'd employed mere moments ago. She lowered herself to her knees and pressed the heel of her hand against his length, molding her fingers around him through the fabric of his suit pants. He had to clamp his eyes shut as that one touch made him even harder than he'd been before, a feat he'd not thought possible.

Metal clattered as she unbuckled his belt, then she unzipped his trousers and he shucked them as fast as he could, tossing them aside. Still on her knees, she slipped her fingers below the waistband of his boxer briefs and slowly tugged them down past his hips. She wrapped her fingers around his erection and stroked, which was already enough to tell him that when he reached his peak, it was going to be earth-shattering. She looked up at him and their gazes connected as she kept her grip on him. Her eyes were intense. They were pure seduction. Then she licked her lips and lowered her head.

As she took him into her mouth, he didn't know whether to watch as she did impossibly sexy things to him or whether he should close his eyes and soak up just how warm and welcoming her lips and tongue were. Nothing had ever felt as good as that. Nothing had managed to be both sweet and hot. She took her time, solely focused on his pleasure. He dug his fingers into her soft hair, caressing gently. Her lips wrapped around him was one of the sexiest things he'd ever seen, but as gratifying as it was, this wasn't how he wanted the next steps of their night to play out. He needed her. All of her.

He reached down and tugged on her arms, and she released him from her lips before he brought her to standing again. He walked her back to the bed and she stretched out on the pale gray duvet, sinking down into the puff of bedclothes. She arched her spine in invitation as he towered over her, his eyes raking over her sumptuous curves. He was ready, right now, to get lost in her.

"Come here," she said, curling her finger.

"Remember when I said I wanted to see more? This is me, seeing more."

She laughed and scooted back until she was in the center of the bed. "Please get a condom."

"So bossy." He reached into the drawer and pulled the foil packet from the box, then tore it open and rolled it on. He placed a knee on the mattress, then another, positioning himself between her curvy thighs. He drove inside, grappling with waves of pleasure…and surprisingly, emotion. He caught himself for an instant, realizing what this meant. He was stepping into the unknown by making love to her tonight. He was going to have to face some obstacles after this, and he'd have to conquer them, too. He wasn't entirely sure of himself in that regard, but Alex gave him strength. She was the reward worth fighting for.

He closed his eyes and focused on the here and now—sensations of heat and pressure building between his legs and in his belly, the sounds of her breaths as they became choppy, and the way her body welcomed his. It was a beautiful thing to be inside her, to have her legs wrapped around him, to know that she was so willing to give herself to him. His peak was fast approaching, but he fought it off, waiting for that moment when Alex finally let go. She was rolling her hips into him, meeting him with every stroke, curling her fingers into his shoulders and digging her heels into the backs of his thighs. She was so close…he could feel her tightening around him, so he lowered his head and sucked one of her nipples hard. It was enough to make her give way, which gave him the freedom to do the same. He followed, taking his most forceful thrust as he finished. As they both began to catch their breath, he settled his face in her neck, inhaling her heady scent. He couldn't escape the feeling that there was something here between them that went beyond attraction or lust. It felt far more consequential than that. And he wanted to think that he was ready to claim it all for himself.

The early morning sun gently nudged Alex from her slumber, and Ryder stirred in bed next to her. He was here. She was here. In his apartment. She could hardly believe it. Her heart reacted first, picking up its pace. Her brain clued in on the activity and went to work, pondering what might be ahead for them. In the immediate future, breakfast was a must. She was absolutely starving. They'd worn each other out last night. But beyond sustenance? A trip back into his bed? An afternoon of making love and simply being alone together? It was everything she'd ever dared to dream of. And now it was all there for the taking.

As if he'd heard her silent ruminations, Ryder rolled to his side and reached for her, his hand curving around her waist and tugging her close. She nestled her face against his chest, not yet ready to open her eyes. She was too busy soaking up the sheer pleasure of being in his arms. His comforting scent, cedar and citrus, filled her lungs. His warmth radiated into her. And all she could do was smile. She couldn't remember being this happy. Ever. Not even when she graduated from college, or the day she opened Flora, even though those days had filled her with optimism and a big sense of accomplishment. Being with Ryder loomed much larger than that. Perhaps it was because for the first time in more than a year, her future again felt boundless and bright.

"Good morning," he muttered, against the top of her head. His fingers brushed along the length of her spine, bringing her whole body alive.

"It's a very good morning."

"Are you hungry?"

"Famished."

He laughed quietly. "I can order something to be delivered."

"Bagels?"

"Whatever you want."

Even the simplest things with Ryder made her happy. This was such a natural and normal back-and-forth. Nothing with Henry had ever been like this. He was always planning the next over-the-top extravagance—it would have been expensive champagne and caviar he'd had smuggled into the country from the Caspian Sea. He was always striving to make each moment more exciting than the last. It was a roller coaster that only went up, and Alex simply wasn't built for that. Bagels in bed with Ryder was her perfect speed.

"I'm on it." He kissed her cheek, then rolled out of bed.

That got Alex to sit up and open her eyes, if only to drink in the vision of his long legs and perfect butt in motion. "Thank you." She scooted back and leaned against his upholstered headboard.

"Of course." He pulled a pair of navy blue pajama pants from his dresser and stepped into them, then raked his fingers into his thick hair as he looked around the room.

This was the best show ever. She could watch it for hours. "Something wrong?"

"Just looking for my phone." He plucked his pants from last night off the floor and pulled the device out of the pocket, then looked at the screen. "Oh. I guess I turned my ringer off. Geoffrey called about a half hour ago."

"I wonder what that's about. Did you leave something at their apartment?"

He grinned. "The only thing I brought was you."

"Well, call him back. Maybe it's good news."

Ryder's face lit up. "You think?"

"It's a definite possibility. Call him."

Ryder pressed the screen a few times and then sat on the bed next to Alex. "Geoffrey. Hi. I'm sorry I missed your call." He glanced at Alex with a sly smile. "I was working on a few things."

She snickered and elbowed him in the ribs.

"Oh, great. Yes. We had a fabulous time last night, too," Ryder said, resting an arm across his belly. "I know. Alex is wonderful. No doubt about that."

Alex smiled even wider. So far, it was a ton of fun to eavesdrop on this conversation.

"Oh, fantastic. That is amazing news. I can't wait to tell Daniel. He'll be so pleased." It was Ryder's turn to elbow Alex.

She grabbed his arm and quietly squealed.

"Yes. Perfect. Friday morning sounds great. Thanks, Geoffrey. I'll tell Alex that Katrina says hi." He listened for another moment. "Okay. Bye." He pressed the red circle on his screen then tossed aside the phone, and looked at Alex, his eyes as big as saucers. "He's coming in. He wants us to pitch him. Daniel and I will get the meeting we wanted."

"That is so amazing. But it doesn't surprise me. I mean, you are brilliant. Of course he wants to work with you."

He knocked his head to one side. "Nothing is decided yet. And I'm not going to argue with you too much about brilliance, but this all coming together is not all me. Nor is it about Daniel or our firm. So much of this has been about you. You're the one who pulled Geoffrey and Katrina in. They were drawn to you. You make everything fun. You're so warm and welcoming. Not like me. I hold back too much."

She took his hand. "That's not true. You're just a little less outgoing than me. Once you came out of your shell a bit, they fell for you, big-time." *Just like I did.*

He leaned closer and planted a soft kiss on her lips. "You just happen to make a particularly good fake girlfriend."

She loved the kiss, but oh, how she hated that word. "Ryder, can we please stop saying fake? It just doesn't seem right to me. Especially after last night."

He narrowed his eyes and the wrinkles in his forehead grew deeper. "I'm not really ready for labels, Alex. This is all pretty new. And I mean, all I'm saying is that you're a very good actress."

He was missing the point entirely and her frustration was growing by the second. "It's not fake to me. Or pretend. Or anything like that. It never has been. And I wasn't acting. Not for a single minute."

"Of course you were."

"I wasn't, Ryder. I was never pretending. Ever. At all."

"That can't be true. What about that first date we went on? The one where you had the photographer tail us? That had to be fake. You had every reason in the world to be mad at me. I left in the middle of the night when we slept together the first time."

Good God, she was so far gone with Ryder it wasn't even funny. "And you kissed me and my anger went away. I look at you and any reasons I ever had for being mad just seem to fade into oblivion. I can't fake it with you. I'm not capable."

"I really don't think that's true."

She had the confession sitting on her lips, the one thing she'd been too afraid to tell him before. But she was so done with hiding things—her feelings *and* the truth. It all had to come out or she was going to burst. "You're the reason I canceled my wedding."

"Wait. What?"

"Ryder, come on. You heard what I said. That day before my wedding, when I ran into you and I started crying? And you comforted me? Then you told me to follow my heart. So I did. That was what made me call it off."

He stood there, frozen, not saying a thing, so she had to keep going.

"You were like this oasis in a sea of chaos. And I know it's hard for you to be open about your feelings, but you are an amazing listener. And I realized then that all of the years I thought I just had a crush on you, that it was so much more than that."

"Years? A crush? On me?"

"Yes, you. You're the one I want, Ryder. From the moment I met you, it's always been you."

"Unbelievable." Ryder got up from the bed and

grabbed a T-shirt out of the dresser and threaded it over his head.

Every bit of confidence she'd had about baring her soul went up in smoke. "What are you saying? Do you think I'm lying? Because I told you I can't hide the truth from you anymore."

"I can't believe you would hide all of this from me. A crush for years? And now you're trying to tell me that I'm the reason you canceled a million-dollar wedding?" His eyes blazed with a surprising mix of fury and hurt. "I can't believe you didn't tell me. I'm now sitting back and looking at our entire history through a different lens. And the last year, is just, wow. You're trying to say that I'm the reason your life is a disaster?"

Her shoulders dropped in disappointment. "It's not a disaster. It's just messy."

"I've heard you use words like that, Alex. It's not just my opinion."

"I really don't understand why you're getting so flipping mad at me. I kept it from you, but it was only because I didn't want to come between you and Daniel."

"And now you're fine with that? You were fine with asking me to blow up my life because you've already done it to yours."

"Wow. Okay. That was a terrible thing to say."

"You put the most important relationship in my life in peril. I entered into our agreement of a fake relationship under pretenses that were themselves entirely false. That's why I let my guard down. I knew that our attraction was going to be an issue, but I figured that we could both be adults about it. But you just kept pushing me and pushing me and wearing me down."

"I seem to remember you enjoying yourself."

"That's beside the point."

Alex had so much frustration built up in her body, she couldn't believe that she hadn't exploded. This wasn't going to go anywhere. She needed space, but he needed time to pull his head out of his ass. "You know what, Ryder? Go fake it with someone else then. Or don't. Just be miserable and lonely and spend your days working too hard and wrapped around my brother's little finger. I can't figure this out for you."

"And I can't figure your life out for you, either, Alex."

"Well, that works out perfectly then, doesn't it? It's all sewn up into a neat little package, just like you like it."

"Don't start with that. Please."

She got up from the bed and gathered her dress and undies from the floor. "The only thing I'm starting is a trip down your hall." She stormed out of his bedroom and marched double time toward his front door.

"You just passed the bathroom," he said.

She didn't turn back. She couldn't go back. She had to go forward. Which meant he could watch her bare ass walk away from him and she'd just have to get dressed in the foyer. Or the elevator. Anywhere to get away from the guy who'd just stomped all over her heart.

Ten

Alex was trying her best to move on from Ryder, but after pining for him for years, then actually having a glimpse of what it was like to be with him, it was going to take a lot more than five days. Yes, she was practiced at the art of wanting him while not having so much as a glimmer of hope. She knew how to function with that burden hanging heavy around her neck. The difference now? She'd had more than a taste of the man she wanted and she knew in her heart that they worked together. They fit together like two pieces of a puzzle. But he'd made his choice. Work and her brother were more important to him. Part of her said that she had to respect his decision, but she was struggling to do that. Mostly because she knew that he was being stubborn and shortsighted. Still, she couldn't figure this out for him. He had to get there on his own.

Time with Taylor and Chloe was the only remedy for her distress over Ryder, so she'd invited them to her apartment for dinner, even if it was a Thursday and not a typical night for them to gather. Preparing the meal seemed like a good distraction, so she'd left Flora for a few hours in the middle of the day and gone to the farmer's market in Union Square to pick up a summer bounty of juicy vine-ripened tomatoes in an assortment of sizes and colors, plus an enormous bundle of aromatic basil and fresh mozzarella for a caprese salad. She'd grabbed a round loaf of crusty bread from a local bakery, and put several bottles of rosé on ice. She'd skipped preparing a dessert, but only because there was a new ice cream place down the street from her apartment and she was eager to try it.

A few minutes before her friends were set to arrive, Alex's phone rang with a call from her mom. She was hesitant to pick it up. Their conversations were seldom short. But they also hadn't talked since Chloe's wedding. "Hi, Mom," she said when she answered.

"Is everything okay? I haven't heard from you. That always makes me worry."

"I'm struggling. I'm not going to lie." She was done putting on a good face for anyone, even her mom, who really preferred it when Alex was happy, sweet and most importantly, willing to acquiesce to whatever her mother wanted.

"Oh, no. What's going on? Can you tell me?"

Frankly, it was refreshing to get actual concern from her mom. It wasn't always the case. "I don't know if I can tell you. It depends on whether you can keep a secret."

"Of course I can."

"Let me be more specific. A secret that tangentially has to do with Daniel. But he can't know about it. Ever. It's better for everyone involved if he never knows." There was no point in telling her brother what had happened. He didn't approve, and it was over between her and Ryder.

"You're really worrying me, honey."

"So, again, let me ask if you can keep this one thing from Daniel for all eternity. I promise you it will only hurt him if he finds out."

"Yes. Go ahead."

Alex took a deep breath for courage, then told her mom the basic gist of what had happened between her and Ryder, that she'd been in love with him forever, and it was never fake to her, and although it was real for a tiny sliver of time, it was over now.

"Honey, are you sure it wasn't just infatuation? I don't know how you could be serious about Ryder. We talked about this at Chloe's wedding."

Alex swallowed hard, readying herself for the final confession. "I was so serious about Ryder that he's the reason I called off the wedding to Henry."

Her mother gasped. "Please don't say that."

"It's the truth, Mom. I'm sorry, but it is."

"That is horrible. What did he do to make you cancel it?"

"He didn't do anything other than be a good friend. And he told me to follow my heart. I didn't love Henry. I never did. Mom, I know you think that you did a good thing by arranging that big birthday party and the public proposal, but it was bad. I was trapped from that moment, and I didn't know how to get out of it."

Her mom's end of the line went so quiet that Alex almost wondered if the call had dropped. But then she finally spoke. "Well, don't I feel like the worst mother ever?"

"That's not what this is. I promise. I love you, Mom. That's part of why I wanted to make you happy. But I have to make myself happy now."

"But honey, it sounds like you aren't actually happy."

Alex tried to look on the bright side. "You know what? I'm not. But at least I tried. I did everything I could to get the guy I wanted to fall in love with me. It didn't work. But again, at least I tried."

"If he doesn't love you, he doesn't deserve you."

"I will tell myself that every day until it stops hurting so much."

"I'm sorry, honey. Truly."

"It's okay. You didn't really like him as my boyfriend, anyway, remember?"

"Well, that was until you told me that he said to follow your heart. Any guy who has the guts to say that to a woman about to get married to someone else at least has some real emotion hiding under that handsome exterior."

Alex sighed. "He is handsome, isn't he?"

"Indeed, he is."

The door to Alex's apartment buzzed. "Shoot. I have to go, Mom. Chloe and Taylor are here."

"Okay, honey. Look, I love you. And don't worry. The person you're meant to be with will find you. I promise. Don't give up hope."

"I'll try not to. Love you, too. Bye." Alex hung up and walked to her door just as it buzzed again. When she opened it, she saw her friends, each with a pronounced look of pity on their face. "Come on in. We can get dinner going."

"How are you holding up?" Chloe asked a few minutes later as she took a seat at the kitchen island.

Alex shrugged as she drizzled olive oil and balsamic vinegar over the platter of sliced tomatoes, herbs and cheese. She wasn't entirely sure how to answer the question. Her feelings were a mess, especially after the conversation with her mom, and she couldn't stop thinking about the other morning at Ryder's and the argument that had ended everything. The loop she was playing in her head nonstop had made her lose all perspective. "I'm devastated. Absolutely gutted." She took a sip of the wine Taylor had poured for them. "But then I'm also not that surprised it didn't work out. Part of me always knew it wasn't going to work out. And now I'm going to have to move ahead. Alone. Possibly forever."

Taylor and Chloe looked at each other, both shaking their heads, making Alex feel even more defeated. Her best friends thought she was as much of a lost cause as she did.

"You're not going to be alone forever," Taylor said. "Ryder has completely messed with your head. I don't think you're seeing this clearly. This doesn't have to be the end. There's a chance he'll come around. And there are always other men."

"You know that's not true for the trust fund tornado." Alex picked up the platter. "Somebody grab the wine. Let's eat." She led the way into her dining room, where she'd already set the table and left out a basket of bread.

"What can we do to help?" Chloe asked as they took their seats.

"Spending time together helps."

Taylor raised her wine for a toast. "To friends."

They clinked their glasses together and Alex tried very hard to fight back the tears. This might not be so difficult if Taylor and Chloe didn't have their romantic futures all figured out. "Thank you both for coming over tonight. It means a lot to me."

"Of course. Anytime. We just hate to see you struggle like this," Chloe said.

"I'm used to it by now. I've been through so many little ups and downs with Ryder over the years. Times when I thought he might be interested. Times when I was sure he wasn't. This was the closest I ever got to being with him. It just hurts to know that it didn't work out."

"Does he know all of this?" Taylor asked.

"He knows most of it. I told him the morning we called it off."

"But does he know the depths of it? Does he know that you've had to endure so much torment because of him?"

"How do I convey that? Plus, it will only make him more mad. He was so angry with me for keeping it to myself. He felt as though I'd violated his trust."

"But is that the reason why you kept that information from him?"

Alex shook her head. "No. I kept my feelings under lock and key because it would have rocked the boat. It would have made things too messy. You guys know me. I don't like to create problems. Even though it seems like I eventually end up creating problems anyway, only later."

"Maybe you need to stop doing that, Alex. You never told Henry how you felt until it was almost too late," Chloe said.

"Look. I totally get that instinct to be polite," Taylor said. "I think we all had it drilled into our heads from a young age. But you can't be afraid to tell people how you feel. And in the case of Ryder, I think you should reach out and tell him exactly that."

"I did tell him. The morning we had our argument."

"Maybe tell him again? Just to be safe?" Chloe reached across and set her hand on Alex's arm. "I hate seeing you so sad. At least if you reach out to him one more time, you'll know that you left no stone unturned."

Alex drew in a deep breath through her nose. "Okay. I'll do it."

Chloe sat back in her chair and took a sip of wine. "Cool. We'll wait."

"What?" Alex asked, incredulous.

"We'll wait. Go call him now. This way we can keep you accountable."

Alex didn't have a whole lot of bravery residing in her body right now, but Chloe and Taylor did make her want to do better. "Okay. I'll be back in a few." She grabbed her phone from the table and ducked down the hall and into her bedroom. She thought about sitting on the bed, but she and Ryder had slept together in that bed, so maybe it would be less painful if she simply wandered over to the window and looked out at the city.

She dialed Ryder's number, her heart threatening to beat its way through her chest. With every ring unanswered, her stomach sank a little lower. Eventually, she got his voicemail. *This is Ryder Carson. Please leave a message and I'll get back to you as soon as I can.*

Taking one deep breath for strength, Alex let it all

go. "Hey. Ryder. It's me. I'm just calling because I feel bad about our argument the other morning. I'm sorry that I hid my true feelings from you. I should have said something. I should have been more transparent about the way I felt." One more cleansing breath was required for the next part. "So, here's me putting it all on the line. I love you. I have loved you for a while now. You're sweet and kind and funny and smart. And more than anything, I feel like myself when I'm with you. We might have been pretending to be boyfriend and girlfriend, but it never felt fake to me. It always felt real. And it's the happiest I've ever been."

Alex turned back to the bed and decided that if she was already being brave, she might as well go in all the way and perch on the edge of the mattress. "If you don't feel the way I do, that's okay. Of course. But I also can't go back to simply being your friend. It will be too hard. And that's all I have to say. The ball is squarely in your court. I know I've used that phrase many times, but it still works. So I'll leave it at that. Goodbye, Ryder. Be well." She lowered the phone to her lap and pressed the red circle to end the call. She didn't feel great about her chances with Ryder, but at least she'd said everything she needed to say. That was far better than she'd done with Henry.

She ambled back into the dining room. "He didn't answer. But I left him a long message. And now we'll just see if he responds. If not, I know that I said everything that needed to be said."

"Good," Taylor said. "We're proud of you."

"Thanks. Now let's finish dinner." She sat at the table and promptly changed the subject. They talked about Taylor's plans with the estate now that Chloe's wedding was over. They discussed Chloe's work life, and Alex's, too. It was so obvious to Alex that her career was going to have to take center stage in her life again, and she had to wonder how Ryder ever enjoyed that feeling. Locked on to it. Perhaps he'd really needed that sense of security, something he hadn't enjoyed growing up. Alex had nothing but compassion for him when it came to that. She'd never endured such a challenge, but she understood it.

When the last of the salad and bread had been eaten, they took the dishes into the kitchen and cleaned up, popping everything into the dishwasher and setting it to run later.

"Anyone want to run down the block for ice cream?" Alex asked as she wiped her hands dry with a dish towel. Yes, her message for Ryder was still heavy on her mind, but sugar might cure that problem for a little while. "There's a new place with all sorts of funky flavors."

Chloe shrugged. "Sure. Why not?"

The three grabbed their purses, then rode the elevator downstairs. They started down the street. It was a warm evening, and the sidewalk was fairly full. Luckily, they were in zero rush, so the three friends took their time.

And then Alex had the surprise of her life. A woman she recognized ducked out of a coffee shop. Alex came to a halt and grabbed Chloe's arm. "Oh, my God. It's Ruby. From the wedding. The caterer who disappeared."

Taylor picked up her walking pace. "Ruby!" she yelled, her voice surprisingly loud.

Sure enough, Ruby turned back. Her eyes went wide with shock, then she whipped around and started hustling away from them.

"Come on, you guys. Hurry up," Taylor pleaded.

The three of them rushed after Ruby, dodging people on the sidewalk as Ruby did the same, zigzagging and ducking down. "She's getting away," Chloe said.

"This is the most absurd thing we have ever done," Taylor said breathlessly.

"Which is saying a lot," Alex quipped, equally struggling for breath, but just as determined to catch Ruby. Something told Alex that she would have answers. Something told her that they had to at least find out what she knew. And if they didn't get to her soon, this chance was going to go up in smoke. Frustrated and panicked, Alex did the only thing she could think to do. She shrieked at the top of her lungs. "Ruby, stop!"

Ruby froze.

For an instant, Alex was in complete shock. It had

actually worked. Then she realized that she probably had a very narrow window of opportunity here. Ruby likely wouldn't stay put for long. Alex scrambled up to her, with Taylor and Chloe in her wake. "Ruby. It's okay. I'm not going to hurt you. I just want to talk to you."

She turned to Alex, her face streaked with tears. "What do you want from me?"

Alex was breathing hard, her brain racing to find the right thing to ask. She had so many questions. But one was the most pressing. "I just want to know something. Are you Little Black Book?"

Her eyes were stormy and wild. "I—I…"

"It's okay. Take a breath. We aren't going to do anything. We just want to talk to you."

Ruby's head dropped and she looked down at the sidewalk. "No. I'm not." Her lower lip quivered when she raised her head again. "My mother is."

Alex reached for Ruby's arm. "Wait. What?"

Ruby was intently focused on Alex, her eyes wide and clear, even when they still welled with tears. "It's my mom."

"Wow. Okay." Of course, this revelation ushered in one million more questions, and she guessed that Taylor and Chloe would have more, too. "Any chance you want some ice cream? We could talk." She pointed to the shop.

"I just want this all to be over."

Chloe stepped closer. "We get it. We do. Let's go

get some ice cream and find a quiet corner so you can tell us whatever it is you're willing to share."

Ruby turned to Alex. "I can trust you?"

She nodded. "You can."

"Okay, then. Let's go."

Alex's heart pounded while her mind raced, but she did her best to stay calm and focused. Inside the ice cream place, she grabbed a booth in the very back while Taylor ordered for them. Once all four were sitting at the table, Alex took it upon herself to get the ball rolling. "What can you tell us?"

"I'm trying to help my mom get what she deserves. Everything she lost because it was stolen from her by her own family."

Alex turned and looked at Chloe and Alex, who were both sitting there in shock. "Do you mean the Astley family?"

Ruby nodded. "Simone Astley was my grandmother. She got pregnant with my mom when she was seventeen." Simone Astley was a well-known socialite who'd died years ago, unmarried and reportedly, with no children. Taylor and Roman had actually sneaked into the run-down Astley estate earlier in the summer, looking for clues after Parker started to sort out the backstory of Little Black Book. "My mom was kicked out of the Baldwell School for Girls and kept at home for the rest of her life. All because she fell in love with a man who refused to take responsibility."

Taylor gasped. "Was it Charles Braker? The English professor at Sedgefield Academy?"

Ruby turned to Taylor, her face painted with shock. "Yes. And your boyfriend, Roman Scott, financed the building that's being built in his honor."

"Everyone you targeted either attended Sedgefield Academy or the Baldwell School. Including us."

"Yes. You know, my grandmother became an outcast. The students and faculty at those schools gossiped about her endlessly. And the daughter she gave birth to, my mother, was treated with the same lack of regard. She was lied to for years. Told that one of the Astley maids was her mother. It wasn't until the maid made a deathbed confession that we found out who my mother's true mom was."

"You guys. This is a lot to go through in an ice cream parlor," Chloe interjected, looking around. "Ruby, would you be willing to come to my office, maybe? So you can tell us everything?"

Ruby shook her head. "I've already said too much. My mom will never forgive me."

Alex couldn't ignore the tremble in Ruby's voice, or the stress that was all over her face. She sensed that everything that happened with Little Black Book was about more than revenge. "Is there something your mom wants? And can we help her get it? Or help you get it for her?"

Ruby looked at Alex with the most perplexed expression Alex had ever seen. "All she wants is what's due to her. But why would you do that? You've all been our targets. We've gone after you all."

Alex had been the victim of so much gossip over the last year, but so had Chloe, Taylor and a lot of other people they all cared about. If she could play a role in ending even a sliver of it, or if she could protect one person from falling prey to it, she had to try. If there was ever a time to rock the boat, this might be it. "It has to stop somewhere. And if we can be a part of that, we're in."

Eleven

Ryder would've been lying if he'd said that he wasn't on edge about having Geoffrey come into the office, even though they already had a great rapport. He felt as though the weight of this meeting rested entirely on his shoulders. If Geoffrey wasn't duly impressed by them as a team, it wouldn't matter that Alex had charmed him so thoroughly. Alex played a huge role in getting Geoffrey in the door, but it was Ryder and Daniel's job to seal the deal.

Despite his worries about the professional ramifications of this meeting, Ryder still couldn't get his mind off Alex. He was not doing well without her. He had very little attention span. All his mind wanted to do was wander over to Alex, dig up a few blistering memories of her, then leave him to ruminate over all of it. To make things worse, she'd left him the most heartbreaking message on his phone last night, professing her love and, as she worded it again, putting the ball squarely in his court. He'd listened to the message a dozen times. And he had not deleted it. He didn't have the heart to get rid of it. She'd been clear that she couldn't go back to being friends with him. It might be the last time he'd ever hear her say nice things to him.

It was an impossible situation, he kept telling himself, but the idea of throwing up his hands didn't make any sense. Still, he was beyond frustrated. Another time and another place? He and Alex would've been perfect for each other. But there was too much standing in the way. Was he really willing to blow up his entire life for a chance at love with Alex? It still felt so risky.

Daniel and Ryder rendezvoused in Reception to wait for Geoffrey a few minutes before he was set to arrive.

"You feel good about this?" Daniel asked.

"I do. He wouldn't have asked for the meeting if he wasn't serious about it. About us."

Daniel nodded and stared at the bank of elevators like he was willing Geoffrey to appear. "Good. Good."

"What do you want me to say when he asks about Alex and me?" Ryder asked.

"Tell him whatever you have to say to get away

from the subject. He's here for a business meeting, not social hour."

"I understand that, but Alex is a big part of the reason we got him in here at all. He's going to ask about her. I know he will."

"Because you guys did such a good job at being a convincing couple?"

"No. Because your sister is an amazing person and people adore her." Ryder was desperate to lower the temperature a little bit. "Look. Even if this doesn't work out, the fact that we're on Geoffrey Burnett's radar is a good thing. It shows that we are operating at the highest levels."

The elevator door dinged, leaving no time for Daniel to give a response, but he did slide Ryder a look that said it would be a complete disaster if they didn't land Geoffrey Burnett as a client.

"Geoffrey." Ryder strode forward and thrust out his hand.

Geoffrey gave Ryder a sturdy shake. "Ryder. It's so good to see you. And you must be Daniel Gold."

"Yes, sir," Daniel said.

"My wife and I are big fans of your sister. She's absolutely lovely."

"That's nice to hear. Thank you," Daniel replied.

"Ryder is a lucky guy," Geoffrey said.

Ryder's stomach sank. He *was* a lucky guy, past tense. Alex might have put the ball in his court, but Daniel was never going to un-dig his heels. "Thanks. I'll take that any day."

The three men strolled into the main office, while Ryder and Daniel gave a brief tour, which ended when they arrived at Daniel's office. Ryder couldn't help but notice the subtle undertones of Daniel's insistence that they meet in his office rather than Ryder's. They might tell people they were equal partners, but there was always a slight edge of disparity between them. Daniel had more power. He was more in control. And Ryder supposed he was entitled to that since it was his family that had put them in the position of opening the firm in the first place. But they were beyond that now. They'd earned their own standing. They'd long since repaid the debt to Daniel's father.

Daniel and Ryder ran through their standard pitch whenever they had a big fish in for a meeting, going through their impressive list of accomplishments, projects and awards. Geoffrey didn't do much more than nod. In fact, it almost worried Ryder that they might be boring him. Alex had already told him most of these details.

"But enough about us. We want to hear more about your needs. What you see the next five years looking like for you," Ryder said.

"Honestly, the big issue for me is trust. I need partners in an architecture firm who will always do right by me. That's part of why I wanted to meet with you both. Ryder, we were able to make that personal connection at Chloe's wedding, and at that dinner at our place. That's been lacking in my business. I'm not getting any younger, and the older I get, it becomes less and less about the bottom line and more about doing quality work with people I enjoy working with." Geoffrey looked at Daniel and at Ryder, then back again. "Meeting Alex was really wonderful, too. Daniel, knowing that she's your sister, and Ryder, knowing that you two are a couple. It just all really brought it into a nice little package for me."

"That's great, Geoffrey. As long as you know that Alex doesn't actually work for us," Daniel said.

Geoffrey laughed and waved away the comment. "Oh, I know that. But she and my wife, Katrina, get along so well. And Ryder, we love seeing you two together. You remind us of the way we were when we'd first fallen in love and couldn't get enough of each other. The other night when you two came over for dinner, you sure had a hard time keeping your hands off each other. That moment when we came out of the kitchen and caught you two kissing in the hall? It was very sweet and genuine."

Ryder shifted in his seat, avoiding eye contact with Daniel. Geoffrey wasn't wrong. He and Alex couldn't get enough. It was just that so much else had gotten in the way. "Alex is an incredible woman. I don't think you'll find anyone in this room who disagrees."

"She seems like the perfect foil for you, Ryder. I sense that she really brings out the fun and upbeat side of your personality. Even now, you are so different from the way you were when you were with Alex.

You're very workmanlike. Serious. And of course, I appreciate that professionalism, but I also know that you can tell a lot about a person when you know the real them. If I had to pick someone to have a beer or a glass of wine with, I'd choose the version of you that you are when you're with Alex."

Ryder felt as though the whole world was slowing down. Again, Geoffrey was dead-on with his assessment of the situation. But Ryder realized just how much Alex truly brought out his best qualities, the parts of himself that he often squashed down because he was in survival mode. But he wasn't back in Boston anymore. He didn't need to merely survive. He needed to live. "I totally understand what you're saying."

"I know we talked about you and Alex getting married when you two came over for dinner the other night, but that wasn't just cocktail conversation. You two are perfect for each other. And if I've learned anything in my years on this earth, it's that you don't pass up a woman like Alex. I hope you'll do something about that soon."

Ryder had no clue what to say in response to that. If he said the truth, Daniel would know what had happened between Alex and him. If he lied, he'd be turning his back on himself, which he'd already done and deeply regretted. "I will see what I can do about fixing that."

"Excellent." Geoffrey got up from the table, prompting both Daniel and Ryder to stand, too. "I think we can work something out here, gentlemen. Let's have you pull together a proposal for the multiuse project I want to do down near the Chelsea Piers. I'll have my office forward the details. We'll look at that and see where we are, but I have a good feeling about it."

"Fantastic. Thank you so much, Geoffrey." Daniel rounded the table and eagerly shook his hand.

"Yes. Of course. Thanks to you both." Geoffrey turned to Ryder. "I feel like a handshake isn't quite enough. Maybe a hug is in order."

Ryder obliged Geoffrey with a quick embrace. "Thank you for coming in today."

"Absolutely. And I meant what I said about Alex. I hope you know that."

"I do, sir. I do."

"Good. Well, I can find my way out. We'll speak soon." In a flash, Geoffrey was gone.

Ryder didn't need to look at Daniel to know that there was something in this room that wasn't quite right. He could feel the negative energy in the air, and he was desperate to change it. "That went well."

"It did. Aside from the talk about Alex. What the hell happened at dinner the other night? He said you couldn't keep your hands off each other."

Ryder greatly disliked Daniel's tone. "That's part and parcel of being a couple."

"What about kissing in the hall? Geoffrey said he and his wife were in the other room. That doesn't sound like faking it. Is there something you need to tell me?"

With every passing second, Ryder felt his blood pressure spiking higher. The anger was boiling up inside him. He loved Daniel like a brother, but he was keeping Ryder from happiness. From true happiness. From Alex. And he was sick of it. So tired of it. He'd been miserable for the last several days without her. He couldn't imagine staring down the rest of his life feeling like this. He'd already had enough. "We need to talk." Ryder walked over and closed the door to Daniel's office. "Things between Alex and I did become real. You just need to know that now. I can't spend the next twenty years working with you and keeping that to myself. And I don't want to lie anymore."

Pure, unadulterated fury was rising in Daniel's face. "Lie *anymore*?"

"Yes. Alex and I slept together at Chloe's wedding. And six months ago, we slept together after that hospital fundraiser I went to. Before that, we kissed at your apartment on New Year's Eve."

"Excuse me?"

Ryder wasn't about to back down now. He loved Daniel and Ryder's entire professional future was tethered to him, but he also needed something real in his life, and Alex held the key to that. "You heard me, Daniel. What Geoffrey and his wife saw between Alex and I was real."

"You slept with my sister? When I expressly told you that I would never forgive you if you did?"

"It was more than sex, Daniel. Way more."

His eyes flared with outrage. "You promised me you wouldn't do that."

Ryder's heart was pumping fast, the adrenaline serving to make him laser focused on what he had to do. He had to end this. Once and for all. "I broke my promise. And I'm sorry. I never should have made the promise in the first place."

"What does that mean?"

"Even before the wedding, what had happened between us was more than sex. And I thought that I could ignore it or will it away, but all it did was grow."

Daniel turned away in a huff and stalked over to the window. "After everything we've been through, I can't believe you would betray me like this."

That word did not sit well with Ryder. "Betray you? Betray *you*? If we're going to talk about betrayal, let's put it all out there. Did you ever stop to think that I might be the one who feels betrayed?"

"How in the hell do *you* feel betrayed? She's *my* sister."

"And you didn't trust your best friend with her heart."

Daniel froze, but did not respond. There was nothing but dead silence. All Ryder could hear was his own heartbeat in his ears. But there was more to be said and he had to keep going.

"You didn't trust me to be a good guy and do the right thing by her. I'm your best friend, Daniel. We have a business together. If you don't trust me to love and care for your sister, then you'll never trust anyone to fill that role. Don't you think Alex deserves better than that? I do."

"Hold on a second." Daniel closed his eyes and pinched the bridge of his nose for an instant. "You said that I didn't trust you to love her. Do you? Love her?"

The answer was right there on Ryder's lips, in his heart and in his head. He'd spent so much time afraid of what Daniel thought and how that might affect the most important relationship in his life. But he'd put all of that on the line and he had to see it through. If this was going to end his friendship and partnership with Daniel, so be it. He had to find a future for himself that went beyond work and career. "Yes, Daniel. I love your sister."

"I don't know what to say to that. Or any of this. It's so much to wrap my head around."

Ryder approached Daniel and looked him square in the eye. "It's very simple. I love your sister. And you told me once that our friendship was stronger than anything. Now it's time to prove it."

Alex was apprehensive about having Katrina come into Flora. She knew there was a very good chance that she would ask about Ryder, and what in the hell was Alex supposed to say? It had been a week since their blowup the morning after they last slept together. Alex was only just now beginning the process of putting the pieces of her heart back together. She wanted to move forward, and talking about Ryder was only going to feel like she was walking in the opposite direction.

She also knew that today was the day Ryder and Daniel were meeting with Geoffrey. The entire friendship Ryder had formed with Geoffrey was born from a time when Geoffrey believed Ryder and Alex were a couple. And Alex didn't think it was a leap to think that Geoffrey and Katrina were both invested in the idea of Ryder and her together. But she was done with faking it. She didn't want to pretend anymore. She couldn't. So today, she would have to tell Katrina the truth. And Ryder would simply have to deal with any fallout on his end. He and Daniel had created the pretense. Let them figure out how to undo it. Alex was done with fixing other people's messes.

Katrina arrived a little after lunchtime, looking every bit the polished and put-together woman she was, wearing slim-fitting white pants with a tailored black blouse and pearl earrings. "Alex, love. It's so good to see you."

Alex embraced her new friend, loving how close they'd gotten in a relatively short period of time. "I'm so glad you're here. I can't wait to hear about your event. Let's go up to my office." She led the way upstairs and offered Katrina a chair opposite her desk. "Please. Have a seat."

Katrina set her designer handbag on the floor and crossed her legs. "So, it's a holiday event to raise scholarship money for the Tisch School of the Arts at NYU in mid-December. I hope this isn't too late. I'm sure you work very far in advance."

"Anything for you. And since it's here in the city, it's definitely not too late. Please, tell me more and then I'll follow up with questions." Alex pulled out a notepad and started scribbling down notes as Katrina shared the details of what she envisioned for the event and what she thought she might need for floral arrangements.

"All I've really thought about is centerpieces, but if there's something else you recommend, I'd love to hear it."

Alex tapped her pen on the desk, thinking. "Swags of greenery are nice that time of year. We could do something over the entrance of the event space. And it might be nice to have more inside. It can really make it smell lovely, which adds so much of a festive atmosphere."

"That sounds fabulous. Really, I trust you. You did such an amazing job with Chloe's wedding."

"I just did the designs. My team did the actual arranging. It's a joint effort."

"Regardless, I love your imagination. It's very impressive."

"Thanks. I appreciate that." Those were the sort of compliments that Alex had once lived for, but they didn't seem to mean as much now that Ryder was out of her life. What did she have to look forward to now? More work? And then more work after that? She certainly had zero chance at romance. The tabloids had made sure of that.

"Is everything okay, Alex? You seem a little off today. Not quite your usual bubbly self."

She sighed. "It's Ryder. He's on my mind. And not in a good way."

Katrina popped forward on her chair. "What? No. What happened? Did you have a fight?"

The old Alex would have downplayed the whole thing. Said something nice to make the entire topic go away. But not the new Alex. She was done being nice for the sake of politeness. "It's over. And you should know that the whole thing was fake." Alex thought about it for an instant—that wasn't entirely true. "Well, it was real for me. But apparently fake for him."

Katrina's eyes narrowed in confusion. "I don't understand."

"I don't want you to think this reflects badly on Ryder. It started out as a favor to me. Ryder agreed to be my date for Chloe's wedding because I was living in fear of negative attention from the tabloids. But the reality is that I've had a thing for Ryder for years. A decade. And so I didn't go into it with quite the same feelings or agenda that he did, even though he thought we did."

"But you two are so great together. I don't see how you could be pretending. I'm a pretty good judge of character at this stage of my life and what I saw looked very real."

Alex sighed, thinking back to the times Katrina had seen Ryder and Alex together. It was one thing to have experienced it herself, but knowing that it looked real? It somehow made the situation even more sad. "It felt so real to me. And honestly, it's the happiest I've been in a really long time. But then he said something about how I was a great actress, I snapped, and I told him everything. I told him that I'd fallen in love with him. And he got really angry."

"Because you fell in love with him?"

"Because we agreed that it would be fake. And I wasn't up-front about my real feelings for him. He said that I put his relationship with my brother in jeopardy."

Katrina sat back in her seat and a concerned sigh left her lips. "Sounds to me like somebody needs to wake up and see the amazing woman that's right in front of him."

"We'll see. I'd love to be optimistic about it, but I'm not holding my breath." Alex's phone lit up with a text. From Jade. Ryder is here to see you. I know you're in a meeting, but he said it's important. Okay to send him up? Suddenly her heart broke out in a flat-out sprint. "Wow. Speak of the devil."

"Ryder?"

"He's downstairs. He wants to come up. What do I say?" As sure as she'd felt of herself a few minutes ago, she was nowhere near that confident now.

"Say yes. I'll get out of your hair."

Alex tapped out a response to Jade. Send him up. "Thanks, Katrina. I appreciate it. I'll email you some design ideas and we can meet about it again to decide the final details."

"That sounds perfect."

"Knock, knock." A sheepish Ryder stood in the doorway to Alex's office. He had a bouquet of tulips in his hand again. This time, they were red.

"Hello, Ryder," Katrina said as she gathered her bag. "I'll let you two talk. Sounds to me like you have a lot to discuss."

Ryder shot Alex a confused look. "Uh. We do?"

"Don't worry, Ryder. Katrina already knows it was fake. You don't have to pretend around her."

Ryder took a step into Alex's office. "Not so fast."

Katrina looked at Alex, then back at Ryder. "I should leave."

"No, Katrina. It's okay. I don't care who hears this." Ryder took another step closer to Alex. Then another. And another. He offered the flowers. "I brought you these to apologize."

Alex hesitantly accepted the bouquet and admired the blooms. There were twice as many as the first time he'd brought her flowers. "They're red. We talked about this. The color of flowers is significant, Ryder. You can't just bring me any color you want." She felt a single tear roll down her cheek and she wished it away. She hated the way her emotions were bubbling to the surface but she couldn't stop them now if she wanted to. She loved him and he was toying with her heart again.

"And I listened to you. Red is for love. And passion. I love you, Alex. And I've been a complete jerk about us."

Katrina sucked in a sharp breath. Alex could relate. She was just as shocked.

"I'm going to *really* take that as my cue to go," Katrina said. "Good luck, you two."

Ryder glanced over his shoulder and watched her leave, then returned his attention to Alex. "I know they're only flowers, but I'm hoping that you'll take them as a token of my affection. And let me keep showing you that affection. I love you, Alex. And I want to make up for lost time."

"First off, *only* flowers? You do know I'm a florist, right?"

He laughed quietly. "I didn't mean it that way."

"Okay. Good." Alex scanned his handsome face—his sculpted jaw, the lips she loved to kiss and the big brown eyes she'd once dared to dream she could wake up next to every morning. "But what about Daniel? I don't want you to cave to his whims, but I also don't want to damage your friendship. Or your partnership. I know how important those two things are to you."

"We talked. And I put it all on the line with him. I told him that you and I were involved, and that he needed to get over it."

Alex blinked several times, trying to imagine

what that scene must have looked like. "And how did that go?"

"Not well. But then I told him how much it hurt that he didn't trust me with you or your heart. I'm his best friend. If he should trust anyone to love and care for his sister, it should be me. And I do love you, Alex. I care for you. I want to be able to care for you for the rest of my life."

Now the tears were really coming, rolling in a steady stream down her cheeks. Yes, Alex had vowed to be strong, but she couldn't stand the idea of being bulletproof when Ryder was opening up his heart to her. She loved hearing these words. It felt as though she'd waited forever to hear them from him, the man she'd wanted from the moment she met him.

"Please don't cry." He wrapped one arm around her waist and pulled her closer as he wiped away a tear with the back of his hand. "I can't stand seeing you unhappy. You know that's my weakness. It was my weakness the day you canceled your wedding."

"Those were tears of misery, Ryder. These are tears of happiness. I love you so much. You have no idea. My heart is bursting just thinking about the things that you just said. I feel like I'm in a dream. The best possible dream. The one where everything turns out and I actually get to be happy."

"It's not a dream, Alex. This is real." He smiled and threaded his hand into her hair, then cupped her jaw and brought her lips to his. That kiss was sheer heaven. The sort of moment that you hold on to forever, until the day you die, because it's just that perfect. "I want to make you happy. I hope you'll let me make you happy," he muttered against her lips.

"You're flirting with me again."

"Damn right I am."

A girlish giggle leaked out of Alex, her heart and body feeling light as air. "You have open license now. Flirt away. All day long. Make me happy."

"What if I want to make you really happy? Like really, really happy?" He reached down and gave her butt a not-so-subtle squeeze.

She laughed and shook her head, unable to hold back the smile that was plastered across her face. "We should probably find some privacy if you want to make me that happy. Your place or mine?"

"I don't really care, Alex. As long as I get to be with you."

Epilogue

Three months later

"Are you sure I can't help? You know that I'm good at stuff like this." Alex was trying really hard to not interfere, but the way Ryder was setting the table for the birthday dinner he'd planned for her was completely wrong.

"Positive. Just go in the other room and relax until your friends get here."

She sucked in a breath when she saw where he'd placed the candles. She would have done something quite different. But this was his gesture for her birthday. And she needed to let go of control.

Thankfully, the doorbell rang, meaning Taylor,

Roman, Chloe and Parker had arrived. Alex rushed to the front door to greet their guests. Taylor and Chloe barged through first, both exclaiming, "Happy Birthday!" in unison. They smothered Alex with a hug, which she was immensely happy to have. Her friends meant the world to her.

"Come on in," Alex said, waving them into Ryder's apartment, which was now officially *their* apartment.

"Hey, you're all here." Ryder emerged from the dining room. "The caterer delivered dinner a few minutes ago. If everyone wants to take a seat, we can go ahead and get started."

He really had done a great job with arranging every little detail, including having food brought in because he was many wonderful things, but he was not a chef. The six of them gathered at the dining table with the oddly spaced candles and started on an impressive meal of beef carpaccio with capers and garlic aioli, followed by a mixed green salad with goat cheese and candied pecans, then seared salmon on a bed of French lentils, bacon and sautéed arugula. Every bite was so delicious. Every course better than the one before it.

"Okay," Taylor said, looking at Alex as they were all finishing up their entrées. "I want to know the latest on Little Black Book. Has everything been worked out?"

Indeed, Alex had been on the front lines of this. After she, Taylor and Chloe ran into Ruby that day on the street, Alex led the charge and talked to Parker about next steps. They found out what Ruby and her mom wanted, then Parker took care of hiring a lawyer to make it happen. "Parker, do you want to tell them?"

"Sure thing." Parker grinned wide. He was immensely proud of the role he'd played in putting an end to the account's reign of terror. "I think you all know that I retained a lawyer for Ruby and her mom. And all they wanted was the estate, which sounds like a lot, but it's honestly a bit of a burden. But I'll get to that in a sec. Anyway, the local historical society has agreed to return the estate and give up the contents of the house. Ruby and her mom agreed to live at the estate and maintain it, and in exchange, the historical society can host two fundraisers there a year."

"I guess they wanted to hold on to that history, right?" Ryder asked. "Ruby and her mom grew up completely detached from their extended family. At least they have the connection of the house and property now."

"I was actually able to help them make one more connection," Roman chimed in. "I think you all know that I was bankrolling the construction of a new building on the Sedgefield Academy campus, and it was to be dedicated to professor Charles Braker, who was one of my favorite teachers. Well, he was the man Simone Astley had the affair with when she was only seventeen. He's Ruby's grandfather. He's her mother's father. I convinced him to talk to them."

Alex gasped. She hadn't heard this part of the story. "What happened?"

"I think it was a little tense at first, but things softened when Charles had a chance to explain himself. The three had quite a nice time and have plans to get together again. He's also set up a fund to help pay for the maintenance of the Astley estate."

"Wow," Ryder said. "That is amazing."

"Wait. There's more," Parker said, looking at Chloe.

She grinned. "This is the real kicker. I hired Ruby to work for my PR firm. She's basically going to be a social media fixer."

"So she'll be using her talents for good?" Alex felt even better about this particular happy ending.

"I realize that her tactics weren't great, but I understand why she was trying to do what she did. What happened to Simone Astley was wrong. What happened to Ruby and her mom was wrong. Three generations of women in that family, kept apart because Simone got pregnant and her mother was embarrassed. It's such a shame," Chloe said.

"I'm sure you've all seen that first post Little Black Book made," Parker said. "It had a picture of a small black diary with the initials SA on it. That was Simone's diary. She kept it while she was pregnant with Ruby's mom. It told the story of how everyone cast her aside, and it named names. Ruby stole it from the house. She broke in the day after she found out who her grandmother was. But that was the genesis of the account. Ruby and her mom didn't have the means to get the estate, so they decided on revenge on the social circles that had wronged Simone."

Chloe leaned into Parker and gazed up at him. "I know that it's been a long and bumpy ride, but even though Little Black Book was an agent of chaos, they played a role in bringing all three couples at this table together."

Silence fell over the group as it all started to sink in. Chloe was right. Little Black Book had done damage, but in the end, it wasn't all bad. In some instances, it was quite good.

"On that note, I think we should have cake." Ryder got up from the table.

"Can I help now?" Alex asked.

"No. But I'll take help from anyone else."

"I'm in." Taylor hopped up from the table.

Several minutes later, Taylor walked out of the kitchen and dimmed the dining room lights. Ryder followed her with an unreasonably large chocolate cake covered in candles. Seeing his handsome face lit up like that, knowing that he'd planned this perfect gathering for her, made it the ideal birthday. Parker started singing "Happy Birthday" and everyone joined in. Well, not really Ryder. He was too busy smiling at her to sing.

"Go ahead. Make a wish," he said when he set down the cake.

In so many ways, her most meaningful wish had

already come true. She leaned down and blew out the candles then planted a big kiss on Ryder's very deserving lips. ˋ

Alex did insist on cutting and serving the cake to Ryder and their guests, then she sat down to enjoy her own slice. It was gone quickly. It had the most heavenly salted-caramel frosting. Then she opened her gifts—a necklace from Taylor and Roman, and a gift certificate for a spa day from Chloe and Parker. Honestly, for Alex, it wasn't about the cake or the gifts, even though she appreciated them very much. It was about this real, relaxed time with people she loved.

After they cleaned up the dishes, they retired to the living room, where they had drinks and a lot of conversation. Ryder, Parker and Roman mostly sat and listened while Taylor, Chloe and Alex told stories, which primarily revolved around giving each other a hard time about foolhardy things they'd done when they were younger. It was great to reminisce. Especially when everyone in that room had a future worth looking forward to.

"We should probably go," Chloe said after consulting her phone more than an hour later. "Our dog, Blue, doesn't like it when we're away for very long."

"Us too," Taylor said. "Roman and I are driving back to Connecticut tonight."

"Working on the estate?" Alex asked. Although Taylor and Roman were enjoying spending time together and working on various projects around the house, Alex thought it also might be that they liked being alone on that big beautiful property. She certainly couldn't blame them.

"A little bit." Taylor glanced at Roman and winked, quite possibly confirming Alex's suspicions.

At the door, Alex gave her dear friends big hugs. "I love you both. I hope you know that."

"We love you, too," Chloe and Taylor said in unison.

Parker shook his head. "You guys. It's not like you aren't going to see each other soon. Or talk on the phone an hour from now. You're inseparable."

"Hey. There's nothing wrong with that," Chloe said. "Absolutely nothing."

They said their final goodbyes and Ryder closed the door. Alex immediately drifted into him. "Thank you for the best birthday ever. It was so wonderful."

He kissed her softly, then took her hand. "But it's not over."

"It isn't? You already gave me my gift." Before everyone had come over that night, he'd given her a beautiful designer laptop bag so she could stylishly ferry her computer to and from the office.

"There's something else I want to give to you. Come on." He led her down the hall and to their bedroom. Alex had recently given it a makeover, bringing in a few feminine touches like prettier bedding and some more colorful artwork. "You sit. I'll be right back."

Ryder disappeared into the closet while Alex wondered what he was doing. "Did you put a car in our closet? Or a puppy?"

He laughed when he came back out, with both hands behind his back. "No. Were you hoping for a dog?"

"Maybe? Not really. But maybe. Some day."

He laughed and strode until he was only about a foot away from her. "Okay. Well, it's not a dog. I went back and forth many times about whether or not to give you this today. I know that your birthday doesn't necessarily hold the best memories."

"Which is why you arranged something very relaxed and intimate with our friends, rather than something with three hundred people. And I couldn't be any more thankful. Really, Ryder, I don't need you to give me another gift." She tugged on his arm. "In fact, you're the only thing I want."

He dropped down to one knee and brought his hands around to the front, revealing that he was holding a small jeweler's box. Alex had seen similar scenes in a million movies, and once from her own point of view, for what ended up being one of the worst days of her life. And although she knew what Ryder was about to do, she had a feeling she didn't know what he was about to say, so she held her breath until he could get out what he wanted to express.

He set the box on the bed next to her and took both of her hands. "Alex, I love you more than I thought it was possible to love someone. And I want to know what you think about getting married. And having kids some day. Plus a dog, apparently. And growing old together."

Alex told herself she wasn't going to cry, but dammit, of course, a single tear just had to roll down her cheek. "Ryder, you know, you almost didn't have to ask. I would love to marry you. You didn't even need to make a big deal of it. You didn't have to go and buy a ring."

"That's not a ring in there." He gestured to the box with a nod. "It's empty. There's no way I would pick out a ring for you without consulting you first. The last guy who did that to you nearly broke you. Which is also why I didn't ask you this question in front of other people. Which is why I didn't make a show of it. I want this to be a partnership. The most important partnership there is."

She reached out and threaded her fingers into his hair, then cupped the side of his face. She couldn't ignore the meaning of what he'd just said. There had been a time when his partnership with her brother was the most important thing in his life. Not anymore. Daniel held a prominent role in both of their lives, but it was the right role, one of brother and friend for Alex, and partner and friend for Ryder.

"I love everything about the way you just asked me to marry you, Ryder Carson. And I can't wait until we get to tie the knot."

* * * * *

#2887 RIVALRY AT PLAY

Texas Cattleman's Club: Ranchers and Rivals
by Nadine Gonzalez

Attorney Alexandra Lattimore isn't looking for love. She's home to help her family—and to escape problems at work. But sparks with former rival Jackson Strom are too hot to resist. Will her secrets keep them from rewriting their past?

#2888 THEIR MARRIAGE BARGAIN

Dynasties: Tech Tycoons • by Shannon McKenna

If biotech tycoon Caleb Moss isn't married soon, he'll lose control of the family company. Ex Tilda Riley's unexpected return could solve his marriage bind—in name only. But can this convenient arrangement withstand the heat between them?

#2889 A COLORADO CLAIM

Return to Catamount • by Joanne Rock

Returning home to defend her inheritance, Lark Barclay is surprised to see her ex-husband, rancher Gibson Vaughn. And Gibson proves hard to ignore. She's out to claim her land, but will he reclaim her heart?

#2890 CROSSING TWO LITTLE LINES

by Joss Wood

When heiress Jamie Bacall and blue-collar billionaire Rowan Cowper meet in an elevator, a hot, no-strings fling ensues. But when Jamie learns she's pregnant, will their relationship cross the line into something more?

#2891 THE NANNY GAME

The Eddington Heirs • by Zuri Day

Running his family's empire is a full-time job, so when a baby is dropped off at his estate, Desmond Eddington needs nanny Ivy Campbell. Escaping painful pasts, neither is open to love, but it's impossible to ignore their attraction...

#2892 BLAME IT ON VEGAS

Bad Billionaires • by Kira Sinclair

Avid card shark Luca Kilpatrick hasn't returned to the casino since Annalise Mercado's family accused him of cheating. But now he's the only one who can catch a thief—if he can resist the chemistry that's too strong to deny...

Finding his father's assistant at an underground fight club, playboy Mason Kane realizes he isn't the only one leading a double life. So he offers Charlotte Westbrook a whirlwind Riviera fling to help her loosen up, but it could cost her job and her heart...

Read on for a sneak peek at
Secret Lives After Hours
by Cynthia St. Aubin

They stood facing each other, the summer heat still radiating up from the sidewalk, the sultry breath of a coming storm sifting through their hair.

Now.

Now was the moment where she would pull out her phone, bring up the ride app. Bid him good-night. If she did this, the past three hours could be bundled into a box neither of them would ever have to open again. He might smile at her secretly every now and then, wink at her in acknowledgment, but that would be the end of it.

If she left now.

"Come up," Mason said.

It wasn't a question. It wasn't even an invitation.

It was an answer.

HDEXP0622

An answer to her own admission in the elevator. That she liked looking at him. That she could look at him more if she wanted.

That he wanted her to.

"Okay," Charlotte said.

Don't miss what happens next in...
Secret Lives After Hours *by Cynthia St. Aubin,*
the next book in The Kane Heirs series!
Available August 2022 wherever
Harlequin Desire books and ebooks are sold.

Harlequin.com